HAYBURNER

Also by Laura Crum

HAYBURNER

LAURA CRUM

THOMAS DUNNE BOOKS
ST. MARTIN'S MINOTAUR
NEW YORK

THOMAS DUNNE BOOKS.
An imprint of St. Martin's Press.

www.minotaurbooks.com

Library of Congress Cataloging-in-Publication Data

Crum, Laura.
        Hayburner : a Gail McCarthy mystery / Laura Crum.—1st. ed.
        p. cm.
        ISBN 0-312-29047-0
        1. McCarthy, Gail (Fictitious character)—Fiction. 2.
Women veterinarians—Fiction. 3. Santa Cruz (Calif.)—
Fiction. 4. Horses—Fiction. 5. Arson—Fiction. I. Title.
PS3553.R76 H39 2003
813'.54—dc21   2002032513

First Edition: February 2003

10 9 8 7 6 5 4 3 2 1

For Andy and Zachariah.
You make my life a happy one.

ACKNOWLEDGMENTS

Thanks to:

Sue Crocker, Wally Evans, Brian Peters, and Todd Brown, who helped train the real Danny;
Craig Evans, DVM, Lieutenant Patty Sapone, and Ray Zachau, who consulted on technical details;
Alycia Weber, who watched Z while I wrote;
Marlies Cocheret, my teacher and friend; and
Andi Rivers, my sister, who has given generous help in many areas over the years.

Grateful thanks also to Henry David Thoreau, always a guide.

Finally and especially, thanks to my grandmother, Jane Richardson Brown, a spirited individual, and my father, Barclay Brown, an equally iconoclastic spirit. I'm glad I inherited your genes.

AUTHOR'S NOTE

This book is a work of fiction. Like all fiction, it borrows from reality. Santa Cruz County is a real place; Harkins Valley is not. And though all the human characters in this book are imaginary, the central crime on which the plot is based did, in fact, take place on my family's ranch, many years ago.

HAYBURNER

ONE

The old barn was a torch. Flames roiled and billowed from the roof, filling the night sky with an orange glow. In the smoky light, human figures ran and shouted, leading and driving shadowy horses. Through the roar of the fire, I could hear loud neighs and shriller equine screams, the crash of shod hooves on asphalt. Fire trucks sat in a row in the drive, and men in yellow suits played hoses in what looked like a futile attempt to douse the inferno. The biggest boarding and training barn in Santa Cruz County was burning.

My God. I had time only for a split second of nightmarish recognition through the windshield before I launched myself out of my pickup truck. Pushing through the crowd in my way, I ducked roughly under the arm of an overweight man who was staring at the blaze with a rapt expression. "Excuse me," I said, "I'm a vet."

I'd taken two fast steps in the direction of the barn when a voice halted me. "Gail, over here."

Turning, I headed toward Clay Bishop, one of the Bishop family—the folks who owned the Bishop Ranch Boarding Stable. Tall, attractive, easygoing, Clay was normally a quiet-spoken, reserved man; he was also a personal friend of mine. I barely recognized his voice, sharp-edged with strain.

"There're a couple of horses in real trouble in the arena. Could you go have a look at them?"

Before I could say yes, he was off in the direction of the barn, long legs shoving him into a run.

Horses in the arena—I took a deep breath. This could be bad. Even as I pushed my way past a group of firefighters with a crisp, "I'm a veterinarian," my mind chanted a repetitive refrain. Take it easy, Gail. Hold it together. Stay calm. Just do what you can do.

"Dr. McCarthy, please, come quick!" A female voice, shrill and panicky. Angie Madison, one of my clients.

I went through the arena gate at a half run; Angie was leading a horse toward me, or trying to. The mare on the end of the lead rope kept planting her feet and coughing violently—deep, wrenching explosions that shook her whole body.

Damn. My mind rapidly catalogued everything I knew about smoke inhalation in horses, which wasn't a whole hell of a lot. This was the first barn fire of my seven-year veterinary career. The big problem, as far as I could remember, was pneumonia. Antibiotics, then.

"She was trapped in there. Bart barely got her out." Tears in Angie's voice.

Bart was Bart Bishop, Clay's brother, and the resident trainer here.

I took a closer look at the mare, and even in the strange orangy half dark, recognized the neat diamond-shaped star on her forehead. Sugar—Angie's horse.

"Will she be okay?" Angie asked, as the mare coughed again.

"Probably." I said it firmly, trying to sound more confident than I felt. "We need to make sure she doesn't get pneumonia."

Even as I checked the mare's vital signs, my eyes roamed the arena. Lots of horses, some loose, some tied, some led by people. All milling about. Whom to help?

Sugar's pulse and respiration were elevated but acceptable under the circumstances, her gum color normal as far as I could tell in the dim light.

"Clay said there were a couple of horses here that were in real trouble?" I asked Angie.

"Oh, yeah. There's two down at the other end of the arena that got burned, I think." Angie's eyes stayed on her mare as she spoke. In her early twenties, she had the egocentricity of youth. Though not unkind, or so I thought, she was incapable of feeling much but the extent of her own tragedy.

"We're supposed to run the barrels at the Cow Palace in another month." Angie watched Sugar heave out another cough. "I guess I'll have to draw out."

"Probably," I said again. "I need to go look at those other horses. Your mare's in no immediate danger. I'll be back to treat her when I can."

"Will she be all right?" Angie asked me anxiously once more. The perennial question.

"I think so," I said. "I'll put her on some antibiotics."

I was moving off as I spoke, headed toward the far end of the arena where two horses were standing. Two human figures held them; another seemed to be applying something to one horse's neck. At a guess, these were my burn victims.

In the periphery of my vision, I was aware of pandemonium around me—smoke and flames bellowing from the barn, choking miasma in the air, a churning mass of people and horses. My mind chattered strange, disconnected asides—damn, it's been a hot and dry autumn; hope this doesn't start another brush fire; let these horses not be too bad.

Still, I kept my eyes focused, ignoring both the turmoil and random thoughts as best I could, moving steadily toward the far end of the arena. I was a vet; this was my job.

"I'm a vet," I said out loud to the woman holding the nearest horse.

"Thank God," she responded.

In the dim light I couldn't see very clearly, but I could smell. The horse smelled of charred hair and burned meat. It stood calmly as another woman applied what appeared to be salve to its neck and withers; I couldn't assess its expression very well, but I knew by the overall demeanor what it would be. Stoic.

I had seen this before in horses with broken legs and other major injuries. Once the initial trauma and panic were past, the horse seemed to withdraw into himself and quietly endure. Nature's way of making the wait for the end more bearable.

"How bad is he hurt?" I said to the woman applying the salve.

"I can't really tell. He's burned pretty bad, I think. He just barely got out. Bart said a burning rafter came down next to him, basically caught his mane on fire." Her voice was calm, almost detached.

"Is he your horse?"

"Yes."

"Would you like me to have a look? I'm Dr. McCarthy from Santa Cruz Equine Practice."

"Of course." The woman glanced at me as she spoke. She was a stranger to me, and I could only guess at her feelings, but despite her apparent detachment, I thought she was on the edge of overwhelm.

I checked the horse's pulse and respiration; both were elevated but not exceptionally so, given the circumstances. He didn't appear to be shocky. His burns, though extensive, seemed less severe than I had expected.

"He's not burned too badly; I think it's mostly superficial," I said to the woman, using the flashlight she handed me to peer at the charred flesh. "That salve is fine to use on him."

"We're lucky," she said flatly. "Two other horses that were right next to him in the barn didn't make it out."

"Oh no," I said.

She merely nodded. "This one," she gestured at the horse next to us, "is burned, too, but not as bad."

I swiveled the flashlight beam onto the horse behind me. The burn marks weren't as extensive here, and mostly over the horse's rump. Once again I did the routine checks and directed the horse's owner to apply dressings and give prophylactic antibiotics.

4

When I was done, someone led another horse up, and then another. Most were coughing; I saw a few more burns. I was just starting to examine horse number six when I heard a familiar voice.

"It is criminal, I tell you, criminal to keep horses like this. See what comes of it."

The voice had a pronounced German accent; I knew to whom it belonged. Hans Schmidt, the new horse vet in town, and a truly flamboyant character. Even a background of smoke and flames couldn't seem to dim his overly charismatic aura. As far as I could tell, he was lecturing the woman next to me on the evils of keeping horses in confinement—a pet peeve of his—while she held a coughing pony who waited for his attention.

"Hans," I yelled, over the hubbub.

"Ah, yes, the lovely Dr. Gail McCarthy." Hans was also an incorrigible flirt. His teeth flashed white in the darkness as he looked my way.

I didn't have the time for this. "Hans, I'm not going to have enough antibiotics in my truck for all the horses who need them. How about you?"

"I have some."

"Could we collaborate?"

"Of course, my dear. What is mine is yours."

"Thanks," I said briefly, not fooled. There would certainly be an accounting later. Hans was as well known for being tight with money as he was for being flirtatious with women.

Finishing up with the horse I was working on, I took a deep breath and dug my cell phone out of my pocket. Pushing one of my speed dial numbers, I waited.

A male voice answered after several rings, sounding both sleepy and annoyed. "Yes?"

"John, this is Gail. I need your help."

"I'm not on call tonight. You are."

"Right. However, this is a major emergency. I've got a fire at the Bishop Ranch and what looks like several dozen horses that need to be started on antibiotics. Could you go by the clinic, load up the other truck, and come out here and help me?"

"It's my weekend off."

"I know that, John. This is a big problem. I need help." I tried to keep the fury I was feeling out of my voice.

There was a moment of silence. Then, "All right, all right. I'll be there." And the click of the phone hanging up.

Damn right you will, you bastard. I stared at the cell phone in my hand, and then shoved it roughly back in my pocket. I still couldn't believe I had to deal with this asshole.

John Romero was our new junior vet. My boss, Jim Leonard, had hired him three months ago, while I was on vacation. We did need the help, and, in theory, I was pleased, though I would have liked to have been part of the hiring process. As it turned out, in practice John Romero was a complete pain in the butt.

Not to Jim, of course. With Jim he was downright obsequious. With me, however, he was hostile and unhelpful, and I had heard through the client grapevine that he bad-mouthed me at every opportunity. Why, I had no idea. He had appeared to resent me from the moment of our meeting, and in the subsequent three months things had gotten worse, not better.

And now, to top it off, Jim was on vacation for a month. With the ballast of his presence removed, John's sulkiness seemed to be leaning toward downright belligerence. I was nominally in charge, but John did everything he could to make things difficult for me, and I simply didn't know what to do about it.

Resolving once again to have a frank talk with Jim as soon as he got back, I started to look at the gray horse in front of me. At the same moment a loud crash startled me into a jerky twist. A sudden gout of flame burst from the barn. Shit. Something had exploded. The air was thick with smoke—my eyes had been running steadily for the last hour, and like my patients, I coughed and hacked.

Momentarily I stared at the barn, mesmerized by the sight. Above the roof, fire reached ever higher into the night. My heart pounded with adrenaline leaking into my system from the sudden start. At the same time I felt a sort of profound wonder. There is something about a big fire that is intensely moving in a primal way. Fear and awe intertwined. I took a deep breath.

Turning back to the gray horse, I began the examination. Focus, Gail, focus.

Two hours later I had treated all the horses brought to me for help. John had arrived with more antibiotics—between us, he, Hans, and I had administered them to all horses who had been trapped in the smoke. As far as I knew, two horses had died, two had moderate burns, a couple had mild burns, and roughly twenty were coughing.

"Is this it?" I asked Bart Bishop, Clay's brother and the manager of the boarding stable.

"Yep." Bart watched me inject penicillin into the last horse's rump. "There were a couple of dozen horses in the big barn."

Bart's voice sounded both exhausted and wired—a combination I recognized in myself.

"How about the other barns?" I asked.

"No problems. They were all metal shed roofs. We got those horses out and away from the big barn and they're all fine."

I turned to look in the direction of Bart's stare, and saw firefighters playing hoses on the charred pile of rubble that was all that remained of the old barn.

"It's a complete loss," Bart said wearily, reading my thought. "And we're underinsured."

For all that I didn't particularly care for Bart Bishop, I felt a rush of sympathy.

"Damn," I said. "Does anyone know what happened?"

"Not really. I got a new load of hay yesterday. You've got to wonder."

It was true. Improperly baled hay had caused plenty of barn fires in its time. Essentially the hay was put up too wet, and the interior of the bale behaved like a compost pile, getting hotter and hotter. If conditions were just right, or just wrong, the hay could catch on fire. Last winter I had opened a bale in my own barn that had steamed heavily into the chilly morning air. The interior was too hot to touch.

I nodded my understanding and felt a hand on my shoulder. "Gail."

It was Clay. I knew his voice and his touch. Turning, I looked up into his eyes—weary, like Bart's, but sadder, it seemed to me.

Clay had beautiful eyes, big, blue-green and long-lashed, under strongly marked brows. Their beauty wasn't particularly apparent now, in the dim light and harsh circumstances, but I was familiar with them from other times and places. Clay's eyes often seemed a little pensive; now they looked positively somber.

"How are the two horses that got burned?" he asked.

"Better than you'd think," I said. "The burns aren't too deep or extensive. I heard you lost two." I looked from one brother to the other.

"Yeah," Bart said. "They were in back, next to the hay. They were trapped back there by the time we saw the fire and started getting the horses out. There wasn't anything we could do."

Clay nodded, not saying anything.

"Bad thing is," Bart went on, "one of them was a real nice show horse, belonged to this woman who spent a lot of money on him. I just hope she doesn't sue us."

I looked at him, thinking the remark a little callous, and reminded yet again of how much I didn't like Bart Bishop. His stance, as always, was somewhat rigid—spine straight, shoulders thrown back, chin up. Despite the exhausted lines around his eyes, visible even in the arena lights, his speech was rapid; in him the adrenaline-wired feeling seemed to be uppermost.

Clay, on the other hand, wasn't saying much of anything, but I could feel his upper arm just touching mine as he stood close to me, as if for comfort. Glancing at him, I saw his eyes were on the ground, not looking at Bart.

"You doing okay?" I asked him quietly.

"I'm fine. Just tired." He met my eyes and reached out to touch my hand at the same time. At the brush of his cool fingers, I was reminded of many other touches, more intimate, at other times. Clay and I had been dancing around the notion of becoming lovers for several months.

And just how do you feel about that, my mind asked dispassionately, registering the touch. Don't know, I answered myself.

Grimacing slightly at this inner dialogue—a habit of mine that

I often wished I could shake—I turned my attention back to Clay. Granted that this handsome, personable man was pleasant to be with and I liked him a lot, I still felt surprisingly detached about him. I could acknowledge my attraction to Clay, but it wasn't driving me.

Another voice jarred me loose from my train of thought. "Is that it?" John Romero. Walking up to me with a characteristic expression and tone—sulky resentment.

"Looks like it," I said as cheerfully as I could manage. "You can go," I added. "And thanks."

To this John merely nodded, then turned and walked away. His surly behavior seemed to penetrate Clay's fog.

"Not really friendly is he?" Clay said.

"He doesn't like me," I said. "I don't know why."

Anything else I might have added was drowned out by Hans Schmidt's voice. "So, Dr. McCarthy, I have a list here for you, of antibiotics I gave to your patients." Hans' teeth shone whitely in the still-smoky night air, his silver-gray hair, neatly coiffed, glowed with some inner moonlight. He looked clean, tidy, and unrumpled—a miracle considering the situation.

I took his list. "Thanks, Hans," I said briefly. Since John had arrived with drugs from our clinic, I hadn't really needed Hans' help. Nonetheless, I had asked, and was now obligated. "I'll have the bookkeeper mail you a check on Monday."

"I thank you," Hans said, sketching a bow. On him the gesture did not appear as ridiculous as one might expect—his courtly manner and flamboyant good looks made it seem natural. At roughly sixty, Hans was a bodybuilder and a triathlete; he was as aggressively fit as many much younger men. And he knew it.

Hans put an arm around my shoulders. "And how are you doing, my dear?"

I wasn't fooled by the pseudo-avuncular stance. Hans was about as avuncular as a great white shark.

"I'm okay," I said. "Rough night for all of us."

Hans squeezed my shoulders. "For a lady, especially."

I stepped quietly out of his arm, looked him in the eye, and said again, "For all of us. But especially for Bart. It's his barn."

Bart and Clay had been watching this exchange without a word. Now Hans met Bart's eyes and I smiled a little to myself. It was no secret that Bart didn't care for Hans Schmidt. Hans had been practicing in the area less than a year, and he had already convinced several of Bart's boarders to take their horses elsewhere, on the grounds that "horses weren't meant to live in confinement." One couldn't expect that Bart would be pleased.

The two men held each other's eyes for a long second; I was reminded of rival male dogs, or perhaps, banty roosters. Bart broke first. Half shrugging, he turned and walked away without a word.

Hans spread his arms. "What can I say? This is what comes of keeping horses in this kind of unnatural confinement."

I'd had enough. "I've heard the speech," I said. "Save it for someone who hasn't." I turned to Clay. "It's been a long night. I think I'll go home and get some sleep."

"You'd better do that," he agreed. It seemed to me there was some underlying emotion in his quiet voice, something I couldn't quite place. Grief? Bewilderment? Whatever it was, I was just too tired to sort it out.

"I'll call you," I said. And left.

TWO

Saturday morning dawned bright, clear, and warm. I lay in bed, looking out my window at the blue sky above the brushy ridge line and wished fervently for clouds and rain. It was early October, and the usual long, dry California summer had been followed by an exceptionally hot, dry fall. There had been no rain as yet, and in the hills of southern Santa Cruz County, this was a big problem.

Little brush fires were becoming increasingly common; all of us hill dwellers lived in dread that one of these would take off. Last night's barn fire had raised that fear in my mind again. The only thing that would make me feel safe was rain, and plenty of it.

But there was to be none of that today, judging by the sky. I booted my dog off my feet and rolled out of bed. Roey, the small, red female Queensland heeler I had just kicked in the ribs, stretched and yawned and followed me to the door.

Letting the dog out, I walked back down the short hall for a cup of coffee. I'd given myself a coffeemaker with an automatic timer for my birthday, and I was really enjoying waking up to the smell of freshly brewed French roast. Not to mention the downright luxury of simply pouring myself a cup, rather than fumbling around in an early-morning daze and then waiting semipatiently for the much-needed beverage to be ready.

Pouring the steaming coffee into my blue willow patterned mug, I added sugar and milk and sat down at one end of the couch. From here, I could see out big windows that faced south and overlooked my garden, and further down the slope, the barn and horse corrals. I watched Roey, prospecting about on her morning rounds, looking very much like a small red fox, and noted that a dozen or so chickens were pecking in my vegetable beds.

The resident pair of banties, Jack and Red, had finally managed to raise a brood. My initial excitement over the tiny, fluffy chicks, hardly any bigger than baby quail, had declined somewhat when Red had decided that her babies needed fresh vegetables. My vegetables. The vegetable garden was fenced, but Red merely flew over, and the walnut-sized chicks just went through.

"Stupid chickens," I said out loud. But I didn't bother to chase them out. They'd only be back in when I wasn't looking. I'd just have to put up with a few pecked tomatoes and lettuces.

Sipping my coffee, I stared out over the garden. Tattered, parched, and dusty as it was, to me it was still beautiful. I had devoted much care and attention when I had planned and planted my border, and used mostly drought-tolerant plants. Born and raised on the coast of California, I was familiar with the difficulty of growing classic British garden perennials in our climate, and had focused largely on Mediterranean plants and California natives, both well adapted to deal with my circumstances.

So the long, wild border that ran beside my drive was thick with rosemary, lavender, santolina, and rockroses, mingling with mounds of still-blooming California poppies, sand verbena, species roses, hardy geraniums, ceanothus, and catmint. And despite the weather and the season, not to mention a complete lack of irrigation, it all looked lively and colorful.

The vegetable garden was, of course, another matter entirely. Tomatoes, peppers, squashes, and the like needed water and plenty of it. They also needed protection from foraging deer, rabbits, ground squirrels, and other predators. Thus my pretty (but not chicken-proof) grape stake picket fence, adorned with climbing tea roses.

My eyes rested on the little fenced garden. The only regularly watered area on my entire property, it was a lush green island of tropical-seeming exuberance surrounded by the olive-drab and silver-gray forms of my Mediterranean plantings. Both vegetables and tea roses luxuriated in raised beds filled with a mix of well-rotted horse manure (from my corrals) and compost, and everything I planted there seemed to flourish, including many fragile creatures that would certainly have succumbed in my wild border.

So, naturally, the vegetable garden was crammed with flowers. Even in October, it blazed with the brilliant oranges of Mexican sunflower, thunbergia, and nasturtium, which contrasted wonderfully with the deep blues of lobelia and morning glory. Cosmos jazzed up the mixture with magenta and creamy white, and the tea roses contributed the more muted colors of their second bloom. All in all, it was a sight to rest the eyes, or I thought so, anyway. The garden, I was finding, gave me endless satisfaction.

However, I wasn't left to contemplate it for long. A shrill nicker broke into my reverie. Plumber was hungry. Getting up, coffee cup in hand, I stepped out on the porch.

Rays of sunlight slanted invitingly through the branches of the big blue gum tree on the eastern ridge, and lit the three still-blooming begonias on my bench. Scarlet, watermelon red, and rich peach, their flamboyant selves were just the accent my plain wooden porch needed and they always lifted my mood.

Carrying my coffee, I headed down the hill to the barn, Roey cavorting at my heels. Three pairs of eyes watched me alertly. My two horses, Gunner and Plumber, nickered happily at my approach, and Daisy the cow lowed plaintively. I fed all three animals a flake of hay, and gave Daisy a pat on the shoulder.

"Today, old girl, you're going home," I told her.

Daisy shied away, uninterested in my words and pats, her focus solely on alfalfa hay. I watched the red-and-white corriente heifer munch and thought that I would miss her. In the year or so I'd owned her, she'd become part of my little animal family.

But change comes to all, and I felt I no longer needed Daisy. I'd purchased her from Glen Bennett, a rancher friend who had used her for team roping, in order to train my younger horse, Plumber, to be a rope horse. Daisy possessed the perfect temperament for.this, and had allowed me to rope her over and over again without "sulling up."

But Plumber had learned as much as he could from this enterprise, and now I had a different project in mind. So I'd called Glen.

"Sure, I'll take her back," he said. "I'll put her in with the bull. See if I can raise some calves out of her."

When I made my second proposition, he'd laughed. "I don't know why not," he told me. "Come on up and get him."

So this morning I was buying a horse. To put it more exactly, I was trading Daisy and some "boot" for an unbroken three-year-old colt.

It wasn't an entirely unpremeditated decision, though in a sense you could call it an impulse buy. I certainly didn't need another horse. But I'd always wanted to break a colt myself, and the opportunity had never come my way. Now I was going to seek the challenge.

Walking back down to the barn, I fed the chickens some hen scratch, which got them out of the vegetable garden, at least temporarily, and gave my old cat, Bonner, a bowl of food. Then I sat on a hay bale awhile, sipping my coffee and watching the animals eat.

Roey snuffled around the haystack, looking for mice. Pale gold early-morning light filtered through the oak trees and dappled the loose straw littered on the barn floor. I could smell the fragrance of wood smoke and ripe apples in the air, the faint and indescribable scent of fall. I smiled. I was happy.

In its own way, this was a small miracle. For the first six months of this year, I'd been in a long tailspin of depression, which had left me exhausted and miserable, unable to find pleasure in anything. Sadly, it had taken a cataclysmic event—the murder of a friend—to jolt me out of my stupor. That, and therapy, and a well-timed trip to Europe had somehow created the necessary change. Now I found myself reaching out to life again, interested and passionate, and just plain happy.

At the thought, I stood up. One of the best things about not being depressed was that I had some energy. Calling Roey to come with me, I started the process of hitching the truck up to the stock trailer.

Two hours later, Daisy was loaded, my breakfast was eaten, and I was ready to go. With Roey grinning happily on the seat beside me, I bumped slowly down my long, graveled driveway and turned left—not an easy maneuver—onto the busy country crossroad I lived on.

My route took me down Harkins Valley Road; passing the house that belonged to my best friend, Kris Griffith, I grimaced sadly at the prominent "For Sale" sign. Kris had moved to San Diego last month, many long hours away, uprooting herself with a suddenness that had surprised both of us. Divorced, single and at a loose end, it had become clear to Kris that change was what she needed—a new job, a new house, a new life. When the opportunity arose, she'd jumped. I wished her well, and missed her a lot.

In another mile I passed the Bishop Ranch; I could see the charred rubble pile where the big barn used to be. Some human figures were moving around, but no one I recognized. Tomorrow, I thought, I'll stop in and have a look at my patients.

Then I was past, with the open, grassy sweeps of Harkins Valley flowing by me and my mind moving on to what lay ahead. Lone Oak and the Bennett Ranch.

The Bennett Ranch was familiar to me from my teens, a time when I was friends with Glen Bennett's daughter, Lisa. She and I had run wild on the place—still a working cattle ranch of nine hundred or so acres. I'd learned to ride on Glen Bennett's team roping horses, and when I finally talked my parents into letting me buy a horse, Glen had sold me one of his retirees, a gentle dark brown gelding named Lad who was both a baby-sitter and a friend.

My friendship with Lisa had waned, though, when my parents

15

were killed in a car crash in my eighteenth year. I'd chosen to put myself through college in order to get a veterinary degree and Lisa had married a rodeo cowboy and moved to Arizona.

We'd met again a couple of years ago, when Lisa, divorced from her cowboy and living on the family ranch, had needed a friend. I'd been there for her as much as I could, and in the process, had renewed my acquaintance with her dad. Now, Lisa was gone again—this time she'd married a man who trained border collies and moved to Oregon—but I was still friends with Glen.

Slowly I wound my way up into the coastal mountains, my pickup significantly hindered by the combined weight of the stock trailer and Daisy. Hot, dry, and dusty, the air that rushed into my open windows was no comfort, nor did the drab, brownish tan of the grass in the meadows rest my eyes.

These fields were bright green in late winter and spring, and a bleached silvery gold that rippled and shimmered with every breeze in midsummer. But now the grass was spent and broken, dulled with dust and sparse at that. Clumps of deep green oak trees dotted the empty rolling pastures; the sky was an unrelieved blue.

Almost an hour after I'd left home, I made it to the town of Lone Oak. A bar/restaurant and a store/gas station with a few houses straggling alongside—that was it. In another minute I was through town and turning into the Bennett Ranch drive. I could see the big weathered gray barns ahead of me—barns that dated from the turn of the last century, and very similar to the Bishop Ranch barn that had burned last night.

Glen Bennett was standing in front of the biggest barn, brushing a bay horse that was tied to the hitching rail. My horse, I thought with a quick thrill of excitement. My colt.

I parked my rig in the barnyard and got out. Daisy mooed questioningly from the trailer, and Roey barked a series of short excited yaps at Glen's black-and-white ranch dog. Glen finished pulling a comb through the bay gelding's tail and stepped back, smiling in my direction.

"Hi, Glen," I said.

"So, how does he look?" he asked.

I ran my eyes over the colt. "He looks good," I said. "Real good."

And he did. Medium-sized for an American Quarter Horse—about 15.1 hands, I thought—and solid dark bay, not a white hair on him, the gelding wasn't pretty; his head was too plain for that. But he was well made and even, everything in proportion, neither overly heavy nor overly light, and he had good bone and nice round feet. Above all, his eye was big and kind and quiet—the sort of horse I liked.

I'd spotted him when I'd purchased Daisy, and asked Glen about him then. But this was the first time I'd seen him since I'd agreed to buy him; the more I looked, the happier I felt.

Glen patted the colt on the shoulder. "Say hi to your new owner, Danny."

"Danny?" I asked.

"That's his registered name. Dannyboy. We always call him Danny. He was born on St. Patrick's Day." Glen smiled.

"Oh." I smiled back, liking the name and the horse equally.

"He's the last one out of my good old mare, you know, Annie," Glen said.

I nodded; I knew.

"She died the next year. This one," he rubbed Danny's forehead, "is a full brother to that Chester horse, that Lonny bought, and the two roan mares I rope on."

I nodded again. I knew. My old boyfriend, Lonny Peterson, was extremely happy with Chester—one of the reasons I'd been interested in Danny.

Glen was talking about Smoke, his stallion and the sire of all these horses. I said nothing, just nodded and let him talk. What I was thinking was how old he looked. Glen Bennett, my childhood idol, suddenly just another old man, rambling on, forgetting that his audience had already heard these stories.

Well, maybe not just another old man. Despite a certain frailty in his stance, and the whiteness of his hair, Glen's eyes were a vivid blue and his voice was strong and animated. In his gestures and body language I could still see the vital cowboy-hatted icon I'd so admired.

My fascination with the cowboy image was waning, though, as I became middle-aged. Surely, I thought, thirty-seven is middle age. In any case, I was finding the allure of men in big hats and boots less apparent; whether it was maturity on my part or merely the fact that I'd known enough cowboys up close and personal that the mystique had just worn off, I didn't know.

I did like Glen, though. For all the semimacho posture that was so much a part of his image, he was a good man, and a kind one.

"How's Pat?" I asked him.

"Real well," he said, with his swift smile. "We're happy."

"That's good." I knew that Glen and Pat, his longtime girlfriend, had recently married, and was glad to hear that things were working out. "Do you hear anything from Lisa or Tim?"

"Both doing well," he said firmly. "Lisa's married a good man this time around. She's fine. And Tim's still training horses over there just a little bit north of Bakersfield. Seems to suit him." Glen met my eyes. "And how are you doing?"

"Good," I said. "Real good."

"Been going roping much?"

"No," I sighed. "I just don't have a lot of free time these days. My job keeps me pretty busy. And then Gunner, you know, that blaze-faced gelding I was roping on, came up lame."

"Damn." Glen shook his head sympathetically.

"Yeah. And my younger horse is still pretty green. He's okay to rope on in the pen at home, but I wouldn't want to take him to a competition."

"You can borrow one of mine."

"Thanks." That was the thing about Glen; he really meant it. I smiled in appreciation, but added, "I'm afraid I'm just not that motivated. I enjoyed going roping when Lonny and I were together, but competing's not really a big deal to me. I like taking my horses for a ride through the hills just as well." We grinned at each other companionably. I'd known Glen and his family long enough that we were almost more like relatives than friends.

"So, do you think I'll do all right, breaking this guy on my own?" I stepped up to Danny and stroked his neck.

"Sure you will," Glen said. "He's a real quiet colt, real easygoing. And all the others were just a piece of cake. No buck in 'em at all."

"That's good," I said. "I'm not sure I could cope with one that bucked."

Glen gave me a look. "Of course, I can't guarantee he won't buck at all. You never know. Do you have anyone to help you?"

"Oh, I can get some help," I told Glen, smiling to myself at the thought of the help I envisioned. Digging in the pocket of my jeans, I produced a folded check and handed it to him. "A thousand dollars," I said. "And Daisy's in the trailer. Promise you'll breed her, now, and not butcher her."

"I promise." Stepping forward, he untied the bay gelding from the hitching rail and handed the lead rope to me. "He's all yours."

THREE

Danny and I got home at about two in the afternoon. I put the colt in his corral and watched him sniff noses with the other two horses; the whole herd trotted about for a while, heads and tails high, giving long rolling snorts. I'm the toughest horse here, each one seemed to say. Of course, since I'd cross-fenced my field into three large corrals, the issue of who really was the toughest couldn't be contested, leaving all horses free to feel comfortably in charge.

I watched the geldings for a while, munching an apple from my Fuji tree and noting with pleasure what a pretty mover Danny was. Gunner, I was not pleased to see, was still slightly lame in his right hind. He'd developed navicular in that foot, a disease that causes degeneration of the small navicular bones, and had been lame for several months. I was treating him for it—so far with no success.

Frowning, I studied the hitch in his getalong, wondering what I ought to try next, both worried and at the same time aware that this was just part of the horse business. My part, actually. As a veterinarian, I was more than familiar with the way horses went inexplicably lame. Sometimes it was fixable, sometimes not.

I would put Gunner back on bute, I decided. Butazolidine was the equivalent of horse aspirin; often a regimen of one gram a day was necessary to keep navicular horses comfortable and sound. Just my luck to have that odd aberration, a horse with navicular in a back foot. Usually navicular disease occurs in the front feet—a back foot is unusual. Still, as I knew, it was far from the worst problem I could have. I would persevere with treatments, and be grateful for the fact that I could give Gunner as much time off as he needed.

Walking over to his corral, I offered Gunner my apple core, which he took with alacrity. I rubbed the underside of his neck and told him what a good horse he was, then turned away. Out of the corner of my eye, I could see Plumber watching me jealously. How, I wondered, was I ever going to find time for three horses; I didn't really have enough time for two.

I didn't know the answer; what I did know was that I was intrigued with the idea of breaking a colt. And as I'd told Glen, I had someone to help me. Or someone who might be willing to help me, anyway.

At the thought, I called Roey and walked up the hill. I had some housecleaning to do before this evening.

Shutting the dog in her pen, I stepped through my front door and surveyed the room. My small house—650 square feet—had one main room that did duty as living room, dining room, office, and kitchen. For a little house, it was a big room, about twenty feet by twenty feet, with another twenty feet to the peak of the open-beam ceiling, so the space didn't seem overly crowded.

One corner was devoted to a built-in desk with a computer on it, one contained a table and chairs, another was wrapped by a terra-cotta tile counter and a stainless steel refrigerator and stove, and the fourth contained a woodstove with a couch in front of it. The center of the room was open, the smooth, polished mahogany-colored wood floor padded and enhanced with a primitive Turkish wool rug in shades of old rose, amethyst, and coffee. At the moment, the rug itself was decorated with a layer of dog hair, as was the floor. Time to get to it; I had company coming over.

21

Removing my pager from my belt, I set it on the table. I was on call this weekend. Mercifully the vicious little black box hadn't beeped once all day, nor had my cell phone rung. After last night's emergency, I felt entitled to a little slack.

Of course, it doesn't always, or even usually, work like that. Some on-call weekends were peaceful, some hectic. This one had begun like—literally—a house on fire, but been quiet ever since. You never knew.

I busied myself with broom and vacuum, then scrubbed the kitchen and the bathroom. The work was enjoyable; I loved this little house. I'd purchased it slightly over two years ago, and its details constantly gave me satisfaction. From the rough golden pine plank walls to the gray stone hearth, to the warm terra-cotta of the tile counters, the house suited me perfectly, and I felt infinitely lucky to have discovered and afforded it.

I liked cleaning the house for visitors; it was a pleasure to show it off at its most beautiful. When the basic chores were done, I plumped up a few cushions, made a marinade and poured it on some skirt steaks, then went out into the garden to pick flowers.

This was the most delightful chore of all, though perhaps more of a challenge in October than at other times. As I stepped out the door, I felt a wave of hot, dusty air hit my skin, and winced. Damn, we needed rain.

Still, there were flowers in the garden. I picked a bouquet of white cosmos and put them in a turquoise glass vase, then brilliant mandarin orange tithonia daisies on long stalks for a big black lacquer jar on the desk. Twining sprays of flame-colored nasturtiums went in a cobalt blue bottle, and a cool green bud vase held one pale apricot Lady Hillingdon rose.

Placing the flowers about the room, I stood back and smiled. The house was what I wanted; it evoked the essence of a dwelling space. Simple, even primitive, in its size and functions, it was nonetheless beautiful and rich in textures and colors. It said what I had to say about home perfectly.

Now, I thought, time for me.

I took a long, leisurely bath, watching the late-afternoon light slant through my west-facing window and illuminate the Italian tile. Eventually, toweled off but with my hair still damp, I stood in front of my antique mirror surveying the clothes in my closet. What to wear?

Something sexy. I stared at the clothes before me. Subtly sexy, not overt. Something appropriate to the occasion. But what?

I held a simple silk sundress in a cool mint green up to my body. The color flattered my dark hair and olive complexion and made my eyes more green than blue; the silk felt great against my skin. Maybe this.

Slipping the dress over my shoulders, I stared into the mirror. I looked good; I had to admit. I'd lost weight during my depression, weight I could stand to lose. Though I would never be described as petite—I'm too tall and broad-shouldered for that—the word slender would not be out of place. I was as fit, trim, and curvy as I had ever been in my life; my small breasts hadn't started to sag and my rear end was firm and round. I smiled.

The smile accentuated the lines around my eyes; my body might look twenty-five, but my face certainly didn't. This was okay with me. I wrinkled my nose and smiled again. This, I thought, is the first time in many years that I've looked kindly at my own reflection. Come to think of it, I couldn't remember ever looking kindly at my reflection. This might be an all-time first.

I paused in the act of combing my wet hair to wonder what had changed. Yes, I'd lost weight, but it was more than that. I had a new acceptance of myself, lines and all. Depression, difficult as it had been, had brought a change that was for the good. Depression and the therapy that went with it and my sojourn in Europe, I thought. All that, and maybe the prospect of tonight's company.

Running my fingers through my hair to ruffle its combed neatness, I smoothed some skin cream on my face and then painted a deep rose lipstick on my mouth. Enough.

I slipped my feet into sandals and headed outside. Afternoon was easing into a warm fall evening as I opened the gate to the vegetable garden. I pulled a carrot for Roey to chew—she loved vegetables—and began to select lettuces, tomatoes, peppers, cucumbers, carrots, and basil for a salad and zucchini, crooknecks, and potatoes to go with the steak. When my basket was full, I carried it up to the house to wash and clean the vegetables. I arranged the salad in a blue-and-white bowl and put the squash and potatoes on the chopping block next to the stove. Flipping the skirt steaks, still basking in their marinade, I went out to the woodpile and gathered some kindling and small pieces of applewood, suitable for a cooking fire, and brought them up to the porch.

As I dumped the ash out of the portable tin barbecue pit, fertilizing the climbing red rose Altissimo, which festooned one pillar of my porch, I stared at the small pond that lay just beyond the railing. This pond was my latest garden project; I'd begun it after I got back from Europe, and completed it a month ago. It had since become my favorite feature in the whole garden.

Of course, gardens are like that. Last year I was obsessed with tea roses; this year with water lilies. Soon it would be garden statuary, perhaps. I never knew what would grip me next. But for the moment, I delighted in my little pond, with its shifting orange-and-white goldfish and one glowing pale yellow Chromatella water lily, just catching the long rays of evening sunlight.

What could be better, I thought, as I built the fire and put a box of matches ready to light it. What could possibly be better than my garden on a golden October evening with a full moon about to rise and company for dinner? My chosen company.

Going back into the house, I took a final look around. The sun shone in through the high window, illuminating a surreal landscape painting on the pine plank wall. I stared. The scene of rolling tawny hills surrounding a cobalt blue water shape took me back in an instant to the Costa Brava. I took a deep breath. The Costa Brava was here with me.

I got tortilla chips and salsa and put them in bowls on the table, found my favorite pitcher and tumblers, of clear sea green Mexican glass with a deep blue rim. As I turned to set them on the counter, I could see a pickup truck coming up my driveway.

Blue was here.

FOUR

Blue Winter, my chosen company, got out of his truck carrying a veritable armful of roses. I held the door open for him, smiling, as he maneuvered both the roses and a brown paper bag that clinked into the room.

"I plundered the display garden," he said, ducking his head a little, and grinning.

"You mean you didn't buy these for me?" I teased, though I knew very well he hadn't. These roses were not the stiff, prim flowers of florist shops; these were opulent, loose, open blooms in the widest possible range of sun-drenched colors—coral red, straw yellow, apricot gold, blush pink.

I lifted one unfamiliar blossom in a rich peach tone and smiled at the unique fragrance—spicy rather than sweet.

"I call that rose Leonie," Blue said, answering my unspoken question. "I can't say her full name, though I'll write it down for you if you want. Too many tea roses have these darn unpronounceable French names." He grinned again, showing slightly crooked teeth and an engaging warmth in his blue-gray eyes.

"Surely a rose grower should speak French." I looked up— Blue was all of six and a half feet tall—and wished I could run my fingers through the red-gold curls that showed under the brim of his gray fedora hat. But we weren't quite on those terms yet.

"I just grow 'em, I don't sell 'em. Somebody else does that." Blue watched as I filled a large clear glass vase with water and began arranging the roses in it. "I know you have plenty of tea roses of your own," he said. "I just thought. . . ."

"No, no," I broke in, "this is great. I almost hate to pick my roses this time of year, there're so few of them. This is a treat."

We smiled at each other, the initial awkwardness of meeting again after a couple of weeks wearing off. Both Blue and I had busy lives; between my veterinary work and his job as a plant breeder and greenhouse manager for a local rose growing company, we'd only managed to get together a few times since I'd come home from Europe. I sensed that our mutual interest was growing, though, and wondered whether we were near that inevitable step into intimacy.

"Can I make you a drink?" he asked.

"You sure can." I gestured at the pitcher and glasses set out on the counter and watched him unpack tequila, orange liqueur, and limes out of his brown paper bag.

Blue began cutting and squeezing the limes; as he had his back to me, I took the opportunity to stare at him a little. Well, maybe lust after him was more accurate. I wanted to run my hands across the broad shoulders, stroke that long back, and then work my way down. Watching Blue's slender fingers as he squeezed lime juice into the pitcher, I imagined those fingers touching me and shivered. Just how long had I been celibate, anyway?

A year, almost. Too long. Blue and I had engaged in a few good-night kisses on our last couple of dates—passion there, but held in on both sides, or so I thought. We were waiting. For what, I wasn't quite sure.

Blue was pouring tequila into the pitcher now; I watched the ritual of cocktail mixing with pleasure. How delightful it was to share this with someone I enjoyed at the end of a sunny fall day.

The pitcher was full and Blue was stirring; ice cubes clinked briskly.

"Shall we sit on the porch?" I asked.

"You bet." Blue poured two glasses full of pale green liquid over ice and followed me out the door. Taking a seat on the bench where I could see the pond, I accepted a glass.

"Here's to you, Stormy," Blue said.

I clinked my glass against his. "Here's to us."

We both drank; the margarita tasted of sweet citrus and salty tequila.

Blue smiled. "*Ahh*. Strong and sweet. Just like I like my women."

I smiled back. "Is that right? Do I qualify?"

Blue met my eyes and sat down next to me; I could feel his shoulder and arm against mine, feel our thighs touching. I tingled everywhere my skin met his.

"You'll do," he said.

We sipped our drinks in silence for a while. For my part, I was wondering what to say. Let's go to bed, seemed a little forward, and I still wasn't sure.

What I finally said was, "I bought a horse today."

"You did?" Blue sounded surprised, whether at my purchase or the new subject, I didn't know.

"Yeah, want to see him?" I stood up; if I didn't remove by body from this close proximity to his, I was going to start pawing the man. It's too early in the evening for that, I told myself as we walked down to the barn, drinks in hand.

I pointed Blue to Danny's corral; we both watched the bay colt walk to meet us. I said, "You told me you've done a lot of work starting colts."

"That's right." Blue was sizing Danny up.

"This guy's an unbroken three-year-old. I'm planning to start him myself and I thought you might give me a few tips."

"Nice colt," Blue said. "I'll help you with him, if you want."

"That would be great. I want to do the actual work myself; I want to be the first one on him, but I could sure use some guidance."

"No problem," Blue said. Judging by his pleased expression as he watched me distribute alfalfa hay, he liked my idea of a shared project as well as I did.

27

I finished feeding the animals; Blue poured us a second round while I lit the fire and chopped the vegetables. "Dinner tonight is all out of my garden," I told him, "with the exception of the steak. I didn't butcher my cow, I want you to know. I just traded her for the colt."

Blue grinned at that and handed me a fresh drink. When our fingers touched, I almost jumped. Damn, the current between us was strong—a real physical jolt.

"So tell me," I said, as I put the potatoes in the steamer, "where did you learn how to start colts?"

Blue was quiet a minute. "Where I grew up," he said at last. "In the Central Valley. I learned from an old man named Tom Billings. He had the ranch next door to us and raised horses. I worked for him for maybe five or six years."

"Starting his colts?" I asked.

"That, and whatever else needed doing. There's always lots on a ranch. I mended fence, dug ditches—you name it. By the time I went to work for Tom he was in his eighties, so even though he was a master at it, he had me get on the colts. His body just couldn't take it anymore."

"So he was a real horse guru?"

"Yeah, he was the real thing. There's a lot of talk about it these days—horse whispering and such. A lot of people making a lot of claims, and taking other people's money. Tom was nothing like that. He didn't make claims and he didn't start colts for anyone else. He'd just been raising and training horses all his life and he knew what they were thinking."

I nodded.

"He taught me how to read a horse," Blue went on. "It's pretty simple, really. Once you understand where a colt is coming from, if you work with him sympathetically, you almost can't go wrong."

"Some are harder than others, though, right?"

"Well, they're all individuals, just like people," Blue said. "And just like people, there are certain basic principles that apply to horses in general, but within that range, there's a lot of variation. Some horses are bold, some are timid, some are cranky, some are playful . . . like that. You have to meet them where they are, just like people, and not project a bunch of your own stuff onto them." He ducked his head and looked down suddenly. "Of course, I'm not telling you anything you don't already know."

I put the squash into the pot and said, "Yes, you are. I understand the part about how horses are individuals, sure, but I've never started a colt before. I'm interested in anything you can tell me."

"It's hard to put in words," Blue said. "At least, it's hard for me. Maybe if I'm just with you while you work with your colt, I can tell you what I see."

"That sounds great," I said. "I'd appreciate it a lot."

"You've set up a round pen." Blue was looking out the window and down the slope toward my small riding arena; I'd used some of my portable metal corral panels to build a fifty-foot circular pen in one corner.

"Yeah. I figured I'd need it." I carried the marinated steaks out on the porch.

"It's the easiest way, I think." Blue watched me prod at the fire and settle the grill on top.

"So, how did you get started working for Tom . . . Billings?" I asked, as I laid the steaks on the grill.

Blue seemed to consider this. "Well, I lived next door. My father raised hay, like a lot of people in those parts, but we didn't have any livestock. I was real interested in horses, so I used to go hang around Tom's place.

"Tom was a funny kind of guy; he wasn't exactly friendly. He'd keep an eye on this ten-year-old kid that was always leaning on his fences, trying to pet the horses, but he didn't talk to me much—just told me to watch my fingers around the colts. But I kept coming over, and after awhile he'd give me little chores to do.

" 'Take this bucket of water to that pen over there,' he'd say. Pretty soon he let me help him feed. And then one day—I'll never forget it—he put me up on one of his broke horses and let me ride. After that I was over there every day."

"I can imagine." I flipped the steaks and took a long swallow of margarita.

"It was sort of a long, slow progression," Blue said. "First he taught me to ride, and then he offered me an after-school job as his ranch hand. I knew my way around the place by then, so I could be some help to him. Finally when I was about fifteen, he let me start getting on the colts."

"You were keen to do it?"

"I was keen to do anything with horses. I'd been watching Tom start colts for years, so I already had a clue." Blue smiled. "Tom taught me everything I know about horses. He taught me to rope, too."

"He was a big part of your life."

"Yeah," Blue nodded slowly. "A big part. In some ways I was closer to him than to my own family."

We both stared at the sputtering steaks. Inwardly, I willed Blue to keep talking. This reticent man had never mentioned his family to me before.

The silence seemed to go on and on. Finally I said, "I never felt terribly close to my parents."

Blue seemed to take the cue as meant. "No. Me either. Nor my brother."

"Was that your whole family?"

"Yeah. How about you?"

"I was an only child," I said. "My parents got killed in a car wreck when I was almost eighteen; I was pretty alone, except for an aunt and a cousin in Michigan."

Blue nodded quietly. "I had one brother," he said. "He was killed in Vietnam."

"Oh." I wasn't sure what to say.

"It was really hard on my parents," he said. "Rich was killed when I was just a kid; he was seven years older than me. I don't think my mom ever got over it."

"Are your parents still alive?"

"Yeah. They are. They sold the old farm; they live in a condo on a golf course now."

"And what about Tom Billings?"

"He died when I was twenty. He didn't have any kids. Some cousin of his inherited the place and just sold it off."

"That must have been sad."

Blue looked down at his feet. "Well, it set me to traveling," he said at last.

I lifted the steaks off the grill and carried them into the house. Blue followed me.

"Could you open this zin?" I asked him, handing him the bottle and corkscrew.

"You bet."

In a minute I had the food on the table and Blue was pouring the wine. I felt a brief inner glow of satisfaction that the meal had come together so handily—nothing raw, nothing burned.

Blue lifted his wineglass. "Here's to your garden."

"Cheers," I said.

For a while we ate and drank and Blue made appropriate comments about how good the food was; eventually I took advantage of a pause to lead the conversation back to his life.

"You've traveled a lot, haven't you?" I asked.

"Quite a bit. For ten years, anyway. Mostly in Europe and Asia. I ended up in Australia, and almost settled there for good."

"That's where you got 'Blue,' right?"

"That's right. All redheads get called Blue or Bluey there."

I smiled. "And women named Gail get called Stormy."

"You got it." Blue smiled back. "All I seem to be doing is talking about myself. How about you? What's going on in your life?"

"Well, let's see. Other than buying Danny," I hesitated, then told Blue about Friday night's barn fire, it being the most exciting event in my recent veterinary career.

"That's too bad," he said when I was done. "I know that old place. And you say two horses were killed?"

"That's right," I said sadly. "It could have been a lot worse. I know when I got out of my truck I was really dreading it. But only two horses had burns, and they weren't too bad. The rest were mostly smoke inhalation problems."

31

Blue nodded. "I know that feeling of dread," he said. "When I was sixteen, a bunch of Tom's horse herd got out on the railroad tracks and the train plowed through them. He called me to come help and I didn't want to go."

"Did you?"

"Yeah, I did. It was bad."

I nodded sympathetically. "That's the worst part of my job. Dealing with horses that are really badly hurt. Especially when I can't help them."

"It just wrings your heart, doesn't it? They seem so innocent in their suffering. It's one of the things that got me interested in Buddhism." Blue turned his wineglass slowly; I stared at his long, graceful hand curved about the dark red wine.

"You told me once that you trained to be a Buddhist monk."

"I did. In Dharmasala. I was with a group of Australians; we were lucky enough to be taught by the senior tutor of the Dalai Lama."

"Wow. I don't know much about Tibetan Buddhism, but surely that's a big deal."

"It was a big deal," Blue said evenly. "Like I said, it was an honor. We were the first Westerners to receive that particular teaching."

"So what turned you against becoming a monk?"

"Women, I guess." Blue smiled at me. "I like women too much."

"En masse?" I smiled back at him.

"No. One at a time."

Blue got up from the table and took my hand; I stood up with him. "Can we go sit on the couch?" he asked.

"Sure."

Still holding my hand, he led me over to the couch in the corner. As we settled into it, I could just see the full moon rising behind the big blue gum tree on the ridge. The next second it was blocked by Blue's face as he leaned toward me.

Our lips touched; I was conscious of a million tiny details— the silvery moonlight flowing in my big window, the warm scent of Blue's skin, the touch of his hand on my back. Then everything was swallowed up in our mouths meeting and exploring each other.

Many long minutes later Blue sat up and met my eyes. Pulling me into him, he smiled. "I've been wanting to do that all night."

"Me, too," I said truthfully, and then we were back together again, learning each other's ways.

Blue slipped his hands under my dress and caressed my back; I rubbed his shoulders gently. I could feel the warmth building between us, could feel myself softening. Everything was touching, feeling, scent and skin. Until my mind said, wait.

Why, my heart answered.

You might get hurt, the mind replied.

For another long moment I wallowed in the physical closeness, my mouth connected to Blue's mouth, my body pressed against his. I could feel the longing deep inside, the intense desire to open up to him. But my mind was unrelenting. Do you really want to go to bed with this guy? What about tomorrow?

Shit. The questions took root; I was losing my ability to concentrate on physical sensation. Gently, I disentangled myself.

Blue looked into my eyes. I could read the longing in his, feel the intensity. He reached out for me again; I held his hand in mine.

"Wait," I said quietly.

"All right."

"I'm sorry to be such a spoilsport, but I'm not sure I'm ready for this."

Blue looked puzzled, as well he might.

"I do want you." I shrugged helplessly. "I guess the simplest way to put it is that I'm not completely comfortable going to bed with someone I'm not in a relationship with."

Blue thought about that a minute. "So how do we get in a relationship?" he asked. "Do I need to promise lifelong fidelity before we sleep together?"

I laughed. "When you put it like that it sounds ridiculous. Still, it's true in a way. I've never been promiscuous. The only men I ever slept with were all my boyfriend at the time, and, yeah, we were in a committed relationship."

Blue sighed, and I could feel the moment slipping away. Damn you, Gail, I cursed myself, why couldn't you just relax and let go for once in your life.

Then he smiled at me. "So how about I court you for a while. So you know I'm really interested in you. I can't promise life-long fidelity at this point, but I can sure wait to go to bed until you're comfortable with it." He reached out his hand and took mine. "I won't quit trying, though. That's part of the courting. I want you to know just how interested I am."

Our mouths met again; it was many long minutes later before we disentangled. I felt chaotic, half caught up in the rush of desire and half afraid to take that final clinching step into intimacy.

"I'm just not ready," I said, somewhat incoherently.

"That's okay." Blue sat up again. Still holding my hand, he added, "I'll go now. Do you want me to come by tomorrow and help you work with your colt?"

"That would be great." I felt a huge surge of gratitude and affection for this man; not only had he accepted my anxieties and restrictions without resentment, he was proffering just the sort of reassurance I needed in his offer to come over tomorrow.

"In the morning then," he said.

"About ten o'clock," I agreed, smiling at him again. "That would be perfect."

But it wasn't to be.

FIVE

At eight o'clock the next morning I got a call from the answering service. One of my patients out at the Bishop Ranch was having severe respiratory symptoms. The owner was afraid he was getting pneumonia.

Once I was out there, I knew, I would need to take at least a brief look at the rest of the barn fire victims. Danny—and Blue—would have to wait.

I called Blue and made my excuses; he seemed to understand. As a farmer, he was familiar with the fact that living creatures don't operate by the clock. Animals, like plants, have their needs and emergencies at often inconvenient times.

Half an hour later I'd done the chores, eaten a hasty bowl of cereal, and was on my way to the Bishop Ranch. Frowning, I saw that the temperature, duly noted by the gauge on my pickup truck, was already in the seventies. It was going to be another hot, dry day. Just what we didn't need.

The meadows and forests of Harkins Valley rushed by me, bright and dewy in the morning sun. Billowing in and out along its length, the valley narrowed in spots to a steep, shadowy canyon filled with redwood trees, and then spread out in broad, grassy flats, dotted with oaks.

The Bishop Ranch Boarding Stable was located in such a flat; across Harkins Valley Road from the stable sat the wide plots of Lushmeadows subdivision, a pricey bunch of spec homes for horse people. Lushmeadows had been part of the original Bishop Ranch; Bart and Clay's mother had sold the land to a developer to make ends meet. As I turned in the Bishop Ranch drive I wondered, not for the first time, if Mrs. Bishop had ever regretted her decision.

The smell of charred wood met me as I got out of the pickup; I could see Bart and several other people standing about near the rubble of the big barn. I walked in their direction. A blond woman with her back to me turned her head and looked over her shoulder; I recognized Detective Jeri Ward of the Santa Cruz County Sheriff's Department. We both smiled.

Jeri and I were friends, of a sort. Or, if not quite friends, we were more than acquaintances. Since she'd acquired a horse this last summer, our relationship had become closer.

"How's ET?" I asked her. "He wasn't in the big barn, was he?" I tried to remember if her old gelding, ET, who was boarded out here, had ever been kept in the barn that had burned.

"No, no," Jeri said. "He's fine. He was in one of these shed rows. No problem there."

"Oh," I said. Putting two and two together, I asked her, "Are you out here because of the fire, then?"

"That's right." Sending what I thought was a significant glance at Bart Bishop, who stood about fifty feet away, talking to an older woman, Jeri knit her brows slightly and then indicated the man on her right. "This is Walt Harvey. He's the fire investigator. Walt, this is Gail McCarthy. She's my horse vet."

"Nice to meet you." Walt Harvey stuck out his hand; I shook it. His hand was small and cool and clammy; I resisted the urge to wipe my own hand off on my jeans afterward.

"So, is this arson, then?" I asked the two of them.

Walt looked at Jeri. Jeri looked at me and nodded. "We think so."

Taking this as permission, or so I assumed, Walt addressed

me directly. "Oh yeah. Definitely arson." He grinned as if he were happy about it.

"How do you know?" I asked.

"Char patterns," he responded laconically. "This fire had more than one source of origin."

I nodded as if I understood, though I didn't really, and thought that Walt Harvey was quite a study in contrasts. Short and stout, he looked like nothing so much as Bozo the clown, with a ruff of curly, reddish brown hair surrounding a bald dome, round, slightly watery blue eyes, pale skin, and a weak chin. In counterpoint to his physical appearance, however, he held himself in an exaggeratedly macho stance—shoulders back, chin up, gut sucked in as much as possible, one hip slightly cocked. To top this off, his clothes were very "western"; he wore Wrangler jeans, boots, and a belt with a fake trophy buckle. I thought he looked downright silly.

Having run with the genuine article, I tend to find wannabe cowboys more than a little ridiculous. No horseman worth his salt would be interested in wearing a trophy buckle he or she hadn't won.

Regarding Walt Harvey with a slightly jaundiced eye, I turned back to Jeri. "Does this mean you'll be investigating?"

"That's right," she said. Once again she looked briefly at Bart Bishop and then our eyes met again.

"Oh," I said, under my breath.

I knew, like everyone else in the world, that the owner of a burned-down building is the first suspect in an arson case.

Turning slightly, so my back was to Bart, I said softly to Jeri, "He said he was underinsured."

She shrugged. "So he says," she said equally softly.

Walt Harvey watched this exchange and then chimed in with, "Guy who did this was probably an amateur. That, or he was real keen to make the fire look like an accident."

"How can you tell?" I asked, genuinely curious.

"Used available materials," he said, reverting to the laconic style. "No propellant."

Once again I nodded as if I understood.

Jeri came to my rescue. "What Walt means is that the fire was started with stuff that was already in the barn—easy enough with a building full of hay. The arsonist didn't use gasoline or any kind of fuel as an accelerant. Most professional arsonists use something of the kind—gets the fire going faster, makes it harder to put out."

Walt grinned at Jeri. "You bet," he said. "Amateurs, like our boy here," he indicated the barn with one hand, "just build a little fire with whatever comes to hand. This one started back in the hay barn."

"Could it have been caused by a hot bale of hay?" I asked.

"Nope." Walt shook his head, round eyes twinkling. "That's what we were supposed to think. But no, the guy lit several candles back in the hay and put little piles of paper around them. I found the hydrocarbon residue."

Jeri nodded slowly and held up a transparent bag. Sure enough, there were two charred candle stubs inside, and some burned shreds of newspaper, marked with wax.

"He probably lit at least a dozen of 'em," Walt Harvey said. "This is what survived. These guys that use candles never expect that, but there's always some residue, and I always find it." He grinned.

"Oh," I said again. Looking at Jeri, I asked, "So what happens now?"

"I investigate," she said briefly. "Which means I need to talk to the owners."

I nodded. "I'd better have a look at my patients. See you."

I turned away, but not without a quick glance in Bart's direction. He met my eyes; both he and the woman he was with were staring right at me. I waved a hand awkwardly at them. "I'm here to see a horse with respiratory problems," I said. "Just thought I'd say hi to Jeri."

"Oh yeah. Our very own Detective Ward is looking into this." Bart bared his teeth briefly at Jeri, who walked forward and addressed the woman standing next to Bart.

"I'm Detective Jeri Ward," she said. "Are you Mrs. Bishop?"

"Yes, I am Doris Bishop." The woman held her chin up, but she looked anxious. I stared at her curiously; I'd never seen Bart and Clay's mother before.

Doris Bishop was short, plump, and gray-haired; she stooped a little and leaned on a cane. According to Clay, she'd been fighting cancer for several years and wasn't strong.

She faced Jeri steadily enough, however, her eyes as watchful as her son's, who stood next to her like a short, stocky pit bull on a leash. Bart and his mother appeared to be quite aware that they were the prime suspects.

Waving again, I turned away. Whatever drama this group was planning to play at, it was none of my business. My business was sick horses.

After a little poking around, I found the man who had called me out. His older gelding was definitely suffering from bronchitis; the horse's respiration was elevated and the animal was coughing frequently. I prescribed a new round of antibiotics and told him to call me if the horse wasn't better in forty-eight hours. Then I rechecked the two horses with significant burns, relieved to find they were doing fine. Three more victims of smoke inhalation were showing signs of bronchitis though, including Angie Madison's mare, Sugar.

"Damn." Angie's young and pretty face contorted with what looked more like annoyance than grief. "I'm going to have to draw out of the Cow Palace. And we had a real chance, too."

"That's too bad," I said.

"You're damn right it is." Staring at Sugar morosely, Angie said, "You know we placed at Salinas this year."

"Wow," I said. The best barrel racing horses in the country competed in the Salinas Rodeo.

"If we'd done well at the Cow Palace, I could have got fifty thousand for this mare."

"Wow," I said again, politely, I hoped. I knew good barrel horses were worth a lot. Nonetheless, I wasn't much impressed with the notion that Angie was more chagrined at her horse's decline as an investment than concerned with the animal's well-being.

"Call me if she's not better in two days," I added, and turned away, almost running into Clay Bishop, who had come up behind me.

Clay put out a hand to steady me; our eyes met. I blushed; I could feel it. "Hi, Clay," I said.

"Gail." Clay gave me a somber look. "They're saying it's arson."

"I know," I said quietly.

Angie watched us curiously. Keeping his hand on my arm, Clay led me a few steps away. Out of the corner of my eye, I saw Angie half shrug and lead Sugar off.

"I think they think Bart did it." Clay's voice, very uncharacteristically, sounded shaky with strain.

My eyes shot to his face. "What do you think?" I asked.

"What do you mean, what do I think?" For a brief second I saw a flash of some very intense anger deep in the blue-green eyes. "Do I think my brother lit the barn on fire, killing two horses in the process, to get the insurance money?"

Recoiling a little, I tried to keep my voice calm. "I take it you don't think so."

"You suppose right." Clay turned away from me abruptly. "I just came by to say hi. I'm taking Freddy for a ride." This last was said almost over his shoulder as he walked away.

"Clay, wait." I started after him. "I'm sorry. I didn't mean to upset you."

Clay kept moving. "No problem," he said, his usual easy tone back in place, at least superficially.

More or less trotting after him, I said, "I know this must be stressful; I really didn't mean to make it worse."

"No problem," he said again.

By this time we'd reached the hitching rail, and Clay was untying his bay gelding, who was already saddled and bridled.

Despite the fact that he looked outwardly calm, I had the sense that Clay's insides were churning, and that my thoughtless question had really upset him. Feeling bad, I tried again. "Where are you off to?"

"Just going for a ride." Clay's tone was cool.

I didn't think about it; the words popped out. "Take me with you."

"Do you really want to go?" Clay looked surprised.

"Yeah. It's supposed to be my day off, after all."

Clay paused in the act of mounting Freddy, then lowered his leg back out of the stirrup and handed the horse's reins to me. "All right," he said. "You ride him."

In a second he was untying the lead rope of a black gelding who also stood saddled and tied to the rail. "I'll take Bart's horse."

"Will he mind?"

"Nope. We have an understanding. Either of us can use the other's horse any time. It comes in handy."

"All right." I adjusted the stirrups on Freddy's saddle to fit me.

Clay mounted the black gelding and looked down at me. "Just be careful getting on and off him," he said. "Don't mess around and hang off him or anything."

"What do you mean?" I asked.

"He's funny about some things—like people or objects sort of chasing him, if you know what I mean. He'll run off. He'll even kick at you."

"Maybe I'd better ride that one." I indicated the black gelding with my hand.

Clay shrugged. "If you want. But Blackjack, here, is a jigger. He won't walk. He drives most people crazy."

"Oh." I nodded. I hated horses that jigged.

"Freddy walks out real well; he won't buck or anything and he's real good outside. Nothing bothers him in that way. He's great on the trail. It's just confinement-type stuff that gets to him—ropes dragging from him, stuff like that."

Clay pointed out a big scar on the horse's right rear pastern. "That was there when I bought him; I think he must have got tangled up in something, probably a barbed wire fence. It must have scared him pretty bad. I don't think he ever got over it."

I looked at Freddy. The bay gelding regarded me in return, head slightly raised, a quiet but mildly wary expression in his

41

eyes. I'd worked on this horse once or twice before for Clay—tubed him with mineral oil one time for a minor colic—and the horse had always seemed sensible enough to me.

As if reading my mind, Clay said, "He's all right in most ways. He's a smart horse and he's got a lot of heart. If you were going to pick a horse to ride from here to Texas, he'd be the one. It's just that certain kinds of things really scare him. He almost kicked my head off once when I got off him in a hurry."

"He did?" I said doubtfully.

Clay laughed. "Don't worry. I'm not trying to scare you. He's really an easy horse to ride down the trail."

"Well, okay," I said. "Just how did he happen to try to kick your head off?"

Clay laughed again. "Oh, some girls were working on goat tying in the arena and they wanted me to give it a try. You know what that is?"

"You stake the goat out and then you run down there on horseback, jump off, and tie the goat up. Sort of a lazy man's version of calf roping, right?"

"Yeah. Anyway, I figured since Freddy came from a ranch in Nevada, he'd probably had a few calves roped off him and could handle this. So I said sure and ran him down there and slid him to a stop in front of the goat. It was when I went to get off of him that I got into trouble.

"Somehow or other, seeing my body go by him in this flying dismount I made pushed his fear button. He jumped sideways like a snake bit him and kicked out so hard he'd have knocked my head off if he'd connected. He just missed me by inches."

"Wow." I looked at Freddy dubiously.

"Don't worry," Clay said again. "He's not difficult to mount or dismount in general. I promise."

"Okay." I gathered the reins, put my left foot in the stirrup, and climbed aboard. Freddy stood like a gentleman.

I patted his shiny red neck, settled my right foot in the off stirrup, and looked at Clay. "Let's go," I said.

SIX

Wе rode up the hill behind the boarding stable, following a dirt road I'd seen before, but never been on. Freddy walked out briskly as we passed some big corrals with mares and foals in them. In another minute we were approaching the main ranch house. Painted barn red with white trim, like the rest of the buildings on the place, it sat at the back of the sloping property, looking down on the whole operation.

I glanced at the house curiously as we went by. This was where Bart lived with his mother. Clay's residence was a much smaller house on the other side of the property, one which had been the foreman's house in the ranch's early days.

I knew, because Clay had told me, that Bart and he were half brothers, and that Bart would inherit the ranch when their mother died, it having belonged to Bart's father. "I'm just a tenant here," Clay had said with a smile. "I pay my rent by doing handyman work for Bart." Clay hadn't seemed to resent his role; since he was a contractor who built houses for a living (he'd built my house), repairing the barns and sheds came easily to him, and as he had said, "It's a good deal for me. I can save all the money I make."

Now we were past the ranch house, still going uphill, moving through a little grove of oaks. I saw a flat alongside the road with a small barn and corral set up—two or three horses in the corrals. Freddy looked toward the horses and nickered; I clucked to him and bumped his sides gently with my legs. He moved out smoothly, just as Clay had said he would.

Clay gestured at the little barn. "That's where Freddy and Blackjack live; Freddy was just talking to his favorite mare. So, how do you like him?"

"Well, he's sure a nice walker."

Clay grinned. "He is that."

I could see Freddy's black-tipped red ears working gently— forward and back, forward and back, as he checked out his surroundings and acknowledged his rider. His walk was quick and rhythmic; I noticed he was already leaving Blackjack behind.

I glanced back over my shoulder at Clay, whose mount was jigging, trying to keep up. "It must be frustrating riding that horse with this one."

"It is," he said. "I think Bart just keeps this horse 'cause he's flashy-looking—impresses the ladies."

Clay trotted Blackjack back up alongside Freddy. The black gelding was certainly flashy enough, I'd give him that. True black is an unusual color in a horse, and Blackjack was jet black with four white socks and a white blaze. Medium-sized, he had a little, Arab-y head and a way of arching his neck while he pranced. Though I disliked horses with the habit of chronic jigging, novice horsemen tend to think it makes a horse look "spirited." I could picture Bart wooing the girls with his fancy, prancing black steed.

"Bart's a real ladies' man, isn't he?" I said idly to Clay.

Clay shrugged. "He always seems to have a girlfriend. Not like me." He looked at me as he said it.

Hastily, I asked, "So who's his latest squeeze?"

"Angie Madison, I think."

"Angie. Geez." I was quite honestly surprised. "She can't be much more than twenty-five. And Bart's what? Forty?"

"Forty-five," Clay said briefly.

"He looks younger," I said. Brother Bart was, in fact, as

flashy-looking as his horse. "But still, Angie's just a baby compared to him."

"He likes 'em young," Clay said. "And I wouldn't worry about Angie. I think she can take care of herself."

"Uh-huh." I nodded.

Our two mounts plodded steadily up the hill. It was warm; Freddy's red neck already had a sheen of sweat on it. I could feel droplets breaking out beneath my bangs.

"I'm sorry I overreacted when we were talking about Bart being suspected of arson," Clay said at last. "I guess I feel a little protective of him. He's had a hard life. He went to Vietnam when he was eighteen, got shot in the leg, came home and married his high school sweetheart. They were both nineteen. It didn't last.

"They had two kids and she got full custody. It about killed Bart. For a few years he was more or less a bum. Then he came back here to help Mom run the boarding stable. Ever since she came down with cancer, it's been way too much for her. Bart takes care of her, runs the business, just does everything. I feel like it's pretty rich, that detective accusing him of burning his own barn down."

"I don't think it's personal," I offered. "If it's arson, the owner is always the first suspect."

"Well, it wasn't Bart," Clay said flatly. "I know him, if anybody does, and he wouldn't do that. Bart acts tough, but it's a lot because of the life he's lived. Going to Vietnam was really hard on him. They put him out there on the front lines, hunting the Viet Cong. I think the hardest part of all is that nothing's ever seemed real to him since. He told me that one time. His life now is like," Clay paused, "a faded, monochromatic print in comparison."

"I've heard that about vets," I said. "its hard to adjust to civilian life, once you've been at war."

"I can understand it," Clay said. "Intellectually, anyway. Though, of course, I've never experienced anything like that. But once you've lived life on the edge, with every moment a matter of life and death, I can see where you'd find ordinary civilized life a little weird. Like a sort of ho-hum fantasy that doesn't bear much resemblance to reality."

"Uh-huh." I nodded again, wondering where this conversation was going. Though I sympathized with Bart's situation, he was sounding more and more unstable by the moment. "Bart said he was underinsured," I ventured.

"He is. He won't get enough money out of that barn to build another, and he's bound to lose all those boarders. That damn German vet was trying to talk a couple of them into moving their horses out to his daughter's ranch. I heard him—yesterday morning."

Clay sounded angry again; I tried a mollifying change of subject. "I've never ridden up this hill before. Where does the road go?"

"More or less to the top of the hill." He indicated a trail I could see branching off to our right. "That goes to the same place, so it's easy to ride a little loop. It takes about half an hour. Are you game?"

"Sure." Now that I was horseback, I was enjoying myself. The hill we were riding up was a north slope, and mostly forested; despite the fact that the temperature was roughly eighty and puffs of dust rose under the horse's every footfall, the shade and a slight breeze made it pleasant.

And then, I thought, looking over at my companion, there was Clay.

Clay was looking away from me; for a second I studied him. His face was calm now, the unusual expression of stress gone; once again I saw the personable man who'd been courting me for several months.

From his blondish brown hair lightly sprinkled with gray, to his blue-green eyes, to his tall, lean body, there was nothing one could fault about Clay Bishop's looks. And I liked him, too. I liked his calm, quiet air, his intelligence, his competence. I just didn't know if I liked him as much as I liked Blue Winter.

You're going to have to decide, Gail, the little niggling voice in my mind said. And pretty soon. I was constitutionally incapable of sleeping with two men at the same time. It might not be against anybody's law, but it just wasn't me, and I knew it.

On we went, and up. Freddy walked smoothly; Blackjack jigged alongside him. Both horses were sweaty. Clay sat Blackjack's jig easily, not saying much, just looking at me from time to time. I felt, as I often did with this man, a sense of quiet companionship.

My mind went back to Blue. I felt companionable with him, too, but perhaps there was a little more edge. I was always so aware of Blue physically that I could never quite relax around him.

So, was that good or bad? Sunlight shafted through a little grove of willows by the trail; I stared at their flickering yellow leaves and then back at Clay. Our eyes met; he smiled quietly.

Damn. I really did like Clay. So just what the heck was I going to do?

The road was growing steeper now; even Freddy's long walk seemed more labored as he plodded. Eucalyptus trees closed ranks on both sides, their tall, pinkish, peeling trunks and long blue-green leaves rustling in every breeze. I could smell the sharp, aromatic, camphorlike scent, feel the air that always seems to move in eucalyptus groves brushing my face.

In another minute we'd reached the top—a wide circular clearing in the eucalyptus forest. Wheeling Freddy, I looked out between the slender, straight trunks back down the way we had come—the dirt road rolling through the hills, the roofs of the boarding stable buildings, the wide meadows of Harkins Valley—all falling away in the distance.

In the foreground, at the edge of the clearing, was a huge, venerable blue gum, much like the one that crowned my ridge at home. Wide and branching, the old many-trussed giant was very different in character from the ranks of telephone-pole–trunked trees that made up the rank and file of the eucalyptus forest.

As I stared at the tree and the view beyond it, Clay rode up next to me and held out his hand. I took it, and he pulled me closer, his mouth reaching for mine. For a second our lips met—I could feel the warmth—and then Freddy leaped sideways, almost dropping me to the ground.

Only the fact that my right hand was resting on the saddle horn saved me. Instinctively I clutched and clung on, recovering my balance a second—and twenty feet—later. Freddy snorted, staring apprehensively at Clay and Blackjack.

"Shit," I said.

"I'm sorry," Clay said ruefully. "I should have known he wouldn't like that. I just wanted to kiss you so much."

I had to smile.

Clay smiled back. "I really didn't mean to get you dumped."

"I survived," I said. "He sure can move quick. Fortunately I've got one of my own who's like this—my old horse, Gunner. I'm used to it."

"That's good. So much for my idea of a romantic moment on horseback, though." Clay turned Blackjack away, indicating a narrow trail that departed between the eucalyptus trunks. "That's the way back."

As I clucked to Freddy and followed Clay, I was conscious of a sense of disappointment. A little interlude of minor passion on horseback sounded like fun to me, too.

Maybe, I told myself, you're just horny. You can't tell which one of these guys you like best because you're just too keen to get in bed with somebody.

The thought made me smile. I'd never seen myself as the sort of woman who was so driven by lust that she couldn't make good choices, but you never know what you'll come to.

Watching the back of Clay's head as he guided Blackjack down the steep trail, I reflected that Clay and Blue were in many ways very alike. Both were tall, quiet men who worked with their hands, both gave the impression of being somewhat solitary, both seemed comfortably confident, both were horsemen. Both, I added to myself, came from families of two brothers— both were the younger brother. And in both cases the older brother had been to Vietnam.

But Blue's brother had been killed, so there the similarities ended. And the two men were different in other ways, too. Physically, Blue was much bigger than Clay—taller, bigger-boned, wider-shouldered. And Clay was a much more conventionally handsome man than Blue; he was the type who would be universally considered "good-looking" by women. Blue's looks were more unusual; some would find him attractive with his red-gold hair, freckled, sun-lined skin, and long bones, but he did not, in general, fit the label "cute."

Leaning back as Freddy picked his way surefootedly down the hill, I felt suddenly that I'd come to a crossroads in my life. I'd put it off as long as I could, gone my own way and continued to be interested in both men, felt my attraction to both of them grow. But I was getting to the end of it. I was ready to be involved with a man again. One man. But which one?

Fixing my eyes on the back of Clay's head, I tried to picture him as my boyfriend. It wasn't hard. Then I thought of Blue. I could picture being with him, too. Try as I might, my mind couldn't find a way to weigh them both up and make a nice, logical choice.

Not to mention, I thought, with an inward eye roll, I had problems enough making that first step into commitment and intimacy. My instinct to protect myself by remaining autonomous and invulnerable went very deep. I had trouble just being comfortable in a relationship, let alone deciding which one to be in.

Still, some part of my being was calling out that it was time to quit stalling around and take the step. I just didn't know which direction to go.

As the horses emerged from the steep, shady eucalyptus forest into a wide meadow, I rode Freddy up alongside Blackjack.

"Eucalyptus groves are interesting, aren't they?" I said conversationally.

Clay nodded.

"Ecological purists don't like them," I went on, "because they're not native and they're allopathic—they kill the native plants. But I grew up with eucalyptus trees, and I'm fond of them. They have such a wild feeling, and they're always talking.

It's really something to be in a eucalyptus grove in a storm."

"I bet," Clay said with a smile, clearly uninterested.

I tried a new subject. "Do you take this horse out riding much?" I patted Freddy's neck.

"Once every couple of weeks, if that. I like to cruise him around back here, but I don't really have the time. It's handy to have him though. Both Bart and I like to go camping and fishing and Bart likes to go hunting. Whenever either of us wants to take a trip, we just bring both horses along. Freddy's good to ride and this one," he looked down at Blackjack, "will carry a pack rig." He grinned over at me. "As you can imagine, Freddy doesn't care to have a pack rig strapped to him, let alone have pack bags hung on his back."

"I can imagine."

We rode along quietly for a while; I could see the roofs of the boarding stable ahead.

Clay looked at me. "Would you like to come over to dinner tonight?"

Caught by surprise, I hesitated and then said, "Sure. That would be nice."

Clay hesitated a moment, too. "It's with my mom and Bart," he said at last. "My mom's having us for Sunday dinner. I'd really be happy if you wanted to come."

"All right," I said slowly. Having dinner with Bart and Mrs. Bishop wasn't exactly my idea of fun, but I had to admit I was curious. "What time?" I asked.

"Oh, come by my place around five," Clay said. "We can have a drink first."

"All right," I told him. "I'll be there."

SEVEN

Five hours and two emergency calls later, I was back at the Bishop Ranch. I'd tended to colicked horses at opposite ends of the county, then rushed home to feed my animals, take a shower, and change clothes in the brief window of time remaining. Now I was about to present myself at Clay's door, dressed and ready.

I'd agonized a bit over my outfit; just how formal were the Bishops likely to be at a family Sunday dinner? In the end, I went with a pair of narrow black linen pants, a simple black cotton-knit shell, and a cream-colored silk blouse unbuttoned and tied at the waist as a jacket. My freshwater pearls and black espadrilles completed the effect. Surely, I told myself, I was appropriate for any sort of dinner party on a warm October evening. As a final nod to possible formality, I tied my hair neatly back with a bit of black velvet at the nape of my neck. Good enough for tea with the queen of England.

Clay's expression when he opened the door left me no doubt that I was dressed appropriately enough. "Gail, you look wonderful." Stepping forward, he kissed me lightly on the cheek.

I smiled, pleased by his appreciation. "How about that drink you promised me? I might need a drink, if I'm going to meet your mother."

"Haven't you met Mom before?" Clay led the way into his boxy little living room.

"Sort of. I saw her this morning. She was with Bart. I was talking to Jeri Ward."

"Oh." Clay was nothing if not quick; I was sure he would assimilate the fact that our meeting had not been exactly a pleasant one. "What would you like to drink?" he added.

"Some sort of light white wine, if you have it."

"Would a Pinot Grigio qualify?"

"Absolutely." I smiled at him, pleased at his choice of wine. Lately I'd been on an anti-Chardonnay kick, and since it had become so trendy, it was often the only white wine people had around.

In a moment Clay emerged from his kitchen carrying two glasses of wine. "Shall we sit on the porch?" he asked.

"Sure." I followed him back out the door, somewhat relieved. Clay's little house, which dated from the turn of the last century, had narrow windows, a low ceiling, and small rooms—sitting inside on such a pretty evening seemed silly.

The front porch was as tiny as the rooms, but there were two folding chairs and a small table. We settled ourselves, screened from the boarding stable by a tangled hedge of old shrubs—lilacs, philadelphus, quince, and roses, it looked like. Even from here I could smell the charred wood of the big barn.

Taking a swallow of my wine, I asked, "How are your mom and Bart dealing with this arson investigation?"

"They're pretty stressed," Clay said. "Bart thinks he knows who did it, and he's really pissed that that lady detective is more interested in investigating him."

"Who does he think it is?" I asked.

"Some neighbor kid," Clay shrugged. "He'll tell you all about it, I'm sure."

"The subject's not taboo, then?"

"Oh no." Clay smiled ruefully. "It's probably the only thing anybody will talk about all night." Taking a swallow of his wine, he set his glass down and reached for my hand. "Thanks for coming, Gail."

I took his hand, and he squeezed gently. I could feel the sense of stress in him—not a vibe I was used to getting from Clay.

"I'm glad to be here," I said, not knowing if it was entirely true.

"Well." Clay raised his eyebrows; lifting his wineglass, he emptied it. "We'd better go."

I followed his example and stood up. "Lead on."

Once again, as we walked up the road toward the main ranch house, Clay took my hand in his. I was conscious of the particular feel of his fingers—slender, a little cool to the touch, the skin smooth and dry. His grip was gentle, and I was comfortable enough, walking hand-in-hand with him; at the same time I was aware that the electricity I felt when Blue Winter touched me was absent here. It felt good to touch Clay, it was entirely pleasant, but that physical thrill was missing.

I had no time to reflect more; Clay was leading me up the steps and through the front door of his mother's house, still holding my hand. Extricating my fingers from his, I patted his arm lightly. However fond I might be of Clay, I was damn well not going to greet Mrs. Bishop hand-in-hand with her son. It smacked of a *fait accompli*, and we were certainly not that. Not as far as I was concerned.

Stepping into the living room, I blinked in surprise. It was white. Plush cream-colored carpet on the floor, oyster-toned drapes against the off-white walls, milky white velvet upholstery on the overstuffed couch and chairs. A glass-topped wrought iron coffee table completed the effect. I blinked again. It was all very Art Deco and thirties-looking, but on a ranch?

Glancing down, I noted a worn and slightly dingy trail across the white carpet, marking the route from the front door to the next room. Just what I would have predicted. Whatever in the world had made Mrs. Bishop select white as the theme for a living room in a ranch house?

Doris Bishop gave no clue. She stood in the middle of her all-white room holding herself erect with an obvious effort. I could see her black cane leaning against an armchair that faced the TV.

Clay was making introductions; I responded politely. Mrs. Bishop and I nodded at each other and smiled.

"It's nice to meet you, Dr. McCarthy. Do have a seat."

I settled myself in a chair near the one I supposed to be hers; Clay chose the couch. I wondered where Brother Bart was.

"What an interesting career, being a veterinarian." Doris Bishop sounded firmly cordial.

"I like it," I said simply. Before I could get anything else out. Bart made his entrance.

And quite the entrance it was. "*Goddammit*, Salty, you son of a bitch, get out." I could hear Bart's voice from the next room one second before Bart himself, following a small, fluffy black dog, burst into the living room.

The black dog did a quick lap around the furniture while Bart stomped after him yelling, "Git"; then the pair exited the way they came in. Clay, Mrs. Bishop, and I retained our places.

In a minute Bart was back. "Mom's dog," he said briefly. "He knows he's not supposed to come in here."

I smiled to myself. No secret as to why the black dog was banned from the white living room.

"No need to curse at him, dear," Mrs. Bishop said reprovingly. "Perhaps, now that you've finally arrived, we can eat."

I glanced at Bart curiously, wondering how he would react to what struck me as a chiding tone in his mother's voice. His face showed nothing; he merely nodded assent and led the way into the next room. One by one, the rest of us followed.

The dining room, I was pleased to see, was a little more casual than the living room, more the environment I would expect of a ranch house. Walls and furniture were wood-toned; the floor was some kind of brownish vinyl. I could see a row of boots by the back door. A tiled bar with cabinets over it partially shielded the kitchen.

Clay and Bart went immediately to what were clearly their accustomed places at the table. Surmising that the seat nearest the kitchen was Mrs. Bishop's, I chose the fourth option.

The table was already set, I saw, and the food in place. The main entrée, which appeared to be stew, sat in some sort of warming plate in the center of the table, surrounded by salad, potatoes, and bread. We all served ourselves and made appropriate approving noises. In the interim I took stock of my company and surroundings.

On closer inspection, Doris Bishop did not seem quite as frail as I had expected. I was more aware of a tenacious strength in the woman than I was of potential weakness. She carried herself very erectly, though it clearly cost her some effort, and she was not, I noticed, using her cane. I was glad I'd dressed up a little for the occasion; Mrs. Bishop's silk blouse and formal cultured pearls were every bit a match for my own.

Bart and Clay wore clean jeans and fresh-looking shirts; neither appeared to have made any other concession to dinner. Bart's shirt was a deep blue that matched his eyes; I watched him ladle stew onto his plate and thought, not for the first time, what a classically handsome man he was.

Bart's dark hair showed no gray; his truly blue eyes were relatively unlined. He had a straight nose, a square chin, and a firm mouth, and was in all ways even-featured. Despite the fact that he was a little short for my taste, which runs to tall in men, he was well-made enough, with wide shoulders and a narrow waist and hips. No, you couldn't fault Brother Bart on looks.

It was his expression that was the problem. In my eyes, anyway. Closed and guarded, Bart's face never seemed to smile. His eyes stayed wary; he bared his teeth from time to time, but without warmth. Given his past, as Clay had explained it, I supposed it was understandable, but I still found Bart difficult.

The object of this scrutiny met my eyes across the table. "So, what did your buddy Detective Jeri Ward have to say this morning?" Again, that brief flash of teeth in what passed with Bart as a smile. "Did she tell you I burned my own barn down?"

There was a sudden hush at the table. As I tried to think of a graceful reply, Mrs. Bishop said with some asperity, "Not your barn, dear, mine."

Bart didn't respond to this, just kept meeting my eyes.

I sighed. "No, she didn't say anything like that. It is pretty much standard procedure to suspect the owner in a case of arson, though."

"That's ridiculous," Doris Bishop said sharply. "We have absolutely no reason to do such a thing."

"I'm sure you don't," I said, in what I hoped was a mollifying tone.

"This young woman is extremely out of line. Wasting time when she should be tracking down the real culprit. Bart is sure he knows who did this thing."

I looked inquiringly at Bart.

"Neighborhood kids," he said laconically. "Three of them have been hanging around a lot. One in particular, kid named Marty, is a real troublemaker. I've caught him stealing Cokes, and once, a six-pack of beer, out of the barn refrigerator. The last time I saw him I ran him off, told him not to set foot on the place again. He threatened me, said I'd be sorry. Not a week later we had this fire. What would you think?"

"I don't know," I said truthfully. "I thought you thought it was the hay."

"Not after what that fire investigator guy told me. Seems like it has to be arson."

I nodded.

"And since I know I didn't do it, I figure the only likely candidate is this kid Marty. But your detective friend is so interested in investigating me, she doesn't even seem to hear what I'm saying. All she wants to know is whether I've got some kind of hidden insurance policy, which I don't, since even she can see that what we're insured for isn't close to what that barn is worth to us in income. And of course, she wants to know exactly where I was that evening."

"You were right here with me," Mrs. Bishop said.

"Yeah, Mom." Bart looked at me. "But of course, I went out and checked around the barns, had a look at all the horses, before I went to bed. I always do."

I believed him. It was just what any conscientious manager of a boarding stable would do.

"Did you see anything?" I asked.

"No." Bart shook his head ruefully. "I wish I could say I did, but I didn't. I didn't actually look in the part where we stack the hay; I had no reason to, but I'm sure I would have noticed if there was a fire going in there. I walked right by it. On the other hand, those kids could have been hiding back there and I never would have seen them."

"Do you think they were?" I asked him.

"I don't know. It's no secret that I check around every evening between nine and ten. Anybody could figure it out. Including those kids. They live right across the street in Lushmeadows. I'm sure they know all my routines." Bart sounded strained and weary as he said it; I could feel his frustration from across the table.

Glancing at Clay, I was surprised to see him looking down at his plate, taking no part in the conversation, not even making eye contact with his brother. Clay had been very quiet ever since we'd walked in here, I'd noticed, only speaking to tell his mother how good the stew was.

Doris Bishop was talking now; I heard her say to Bart in what was meant to be an aside, "If you'd only be clear with this detective, dear, and explain what you mean, I'm sure she'll understand."

Taking a final bite of my stew, I leaned back in my chair.

"Finish your stew, dear," Mrs. Bishop said to Bart. "And try to get a little more sleep tonight. You look tired."

I felt like ducking, as if a barbed arrow of a comment might impale me, if I got in the way. No wonder Clay was quiet.

Bart continued to give no sign that his mother bothered him. He finished his stew as directed and rose obediently when she admonished him that the table needed clearing, all without a word.

Once we were settled in our places with apple cake and ice cream in front of us, I asked another question. "Are you worried about these kids trying it again?" I addressed myself mostly to Bart, but included the room at large.

"Do you suppose they will?" Doris Bishop's sharp, querulous tone sounded even shriller with surprise.

"Hard to say." Bart met my eyes. "But I'm ready for them."

"What do you mean?" I asked him.

"I carry a pistol when I do the nighttime check now."

"Is it loaded?"

"Of course."

"Isn't that kind of dangerous?" I asked him. "Surely you don't want to shoot those kids?"

"I'm not a fool." Bart gave me a level look. "And I know about guns. There's no shell in the chamber, and none in the next slot either. I only keep four bullets in the gun. That way, no matter what happens, no one can get shot accidentally."

"Sure," I said. "I did the same thing myself, when I went packing in the Sierras. But what if you catch these kids in the act?"

"Then I figure the gun will help me keep them here until I get your lady friend, the detective." Bart bared his teeth at me again. "I carry a cell phone, too."

I nodded. It all made sense. Still, it struck me that Brother Bart was wound pretty tight. I wouldn't want to be the one to run into him after dark.

Taking another bite of my cake, I readied myself to compliment Mrs. Bishop on her home-cooked food. Before I could get my mouth open, my own cell phone rang.

"I'm sorry," I said. "I need to answer this. I'm on call."

I carried the little phone out into the all-white living room to answer it. In a minute I'd ascertained that I had yet another colic to deal with. It wasn't really a surprise. Colics were our most frequent emergency call, and also the most frequent cause of equine death. A horse's digestive system is in some senses poorly constructed; it can't throw up. Thus any sort of bellyache, known generically to horsemen as colic, could be the cause of a twisted or ruptured gut and a resulting fatality.

Fortunately all the Bishops were horsemen; there was no need for lengthy explanations. When I said I had an emergency colic and needed to leave immediately, the whole group nodded in understanding. I thanked Mrs. Bishop for the dinner and said good-bye to Bart. Clay walked me out to my truck.

"Thank you for a nice evening," I said as I got into the cab.

"I'm not sure about that," he responded. "But I'm grateful to you for coming." And he leaned forward and kissed me.

It was our most lingering kiss yet; Clay's mouth was warm on mine; I could feel his desire. When we parted, he met my eyes. "I think I love you."

I didn't know what to say. Instead, I reached out and gave his hand a squeeze. "See you soon," I told him.

And then I was on my way to yet another colicked horse.

EIGHT

At seven the next morning I was down at the clinic. With Jim gone, I needed to be there early to keep up on things. It didn't help that I hadn't gotten home until well after midnight, or that I'd had to put the colicked horse down. Not a good start to the week.

And things went from bad to worse the minute John Romero walked through the door. Everything about him, from his cocky stance to the sulky expression in his eyes, irritated me.

I just couldn't understand what was going on with this guy. In his late twenties or thereabouts, John had the olive skin and dark hair and eyes that went with his last name, as well as a prominent nose and pouting lips. He looked just what I imagined a young Sicilian gangster ought to look like. Certainly most women would think him handsome.

I had witnessed John doing some very competent veterinary work; the client grapevine reported that he was always polite, though a tad too reserved for some people's taste. Jim seemed to like him. There was no obvious reason for him to have a chip on his shoulder. But as far as I could tell, John had only to look at me to get in a bad mood.

"I expect to be compensated for Friday night." The first words out of his mouth.

"I'm sure you will be," I said evenly. "Talk to Jim when he gets back."

John glared at me. We both knew he wouldn't want to raise the subject with Jim. Helping out in large-scale emergencies was taken for granted. As I understood it, John wanted to keep his position here and was quite keen to get Jim on his side. What I couldn't grasp was why John was so overtly hostile to me. I was a partner in the business, albeit the junior one. Still, if I made enough noise about it, I was pretty sure that Jim would agree to replace John with someone I could get along with.

So why in hell was John going out of his way to antagonize me?

No ready answer sprang to mind, except that it did seem to be a knee-jerk reaction. Perhaps just the fact that I was a woman in a position of authority over him annoyed the man.

I watched John's back move away as he checked his morning calls with the receptionist and knew I had no choice except to try and get along with him until Jim came back. The practice was too busy for one vet to handle it all.

However, we could, I thought, get by with two. Jim had hired John before Hans Schmidt came to town. And Hans had already drawn away a significant number of our clients. Who knew how many more would follow?

Speak of the devil. Nancy, the receptionist, was paging me. "Dr. Schmidt on the phone for you, Gail."

I picked up the extension in my office. "Hello, Hans."

"Good morning to you, my dear."

"So, what's up?"

"It is several things. First of all, you will not forget to submit my bill for antibiotics to your bookkeeper?"

"Nope."

"Of course not. And then, my dear, I have a question for you."

"Shoot." I wished Hans would get to the point.

"I wish to be gracious about this." Hans paused. "I do not quite know how to say it."

"Just fire away, Hans. You know how it is. I've got a full day of calls ahead of me."

"Of course. I have a new client who was at one time your client, and I'm afraid I need the X rays you have taken of this horse."

"No problem," I said crisply. "Who is it?"

"Mary Sinclair."

"Right," I said. "I'll send the entire file over to your office." I tried to sound dispassionate, but inwardly I was seething. Mary Sinclair had been a client of mine for many years. How in the world had Hans managed to entice her away?

He didn't leave me guessing. "I met her at the barn fire. She boards her horse at the Bishop Ranch. Of course, you know."

Of course I know, you bastard, I thought but didn't say.

"Or rather," Hans went on, "she used to board her horse there. She is moving him to Quail Run Ranch today."

"No doubt you talked her into that."

"I suggested it, yes. I feel it will be very helpful for her horse's foot problem."

I could feel the steam coming out my ears. This was Hans' m.o. Quail Run Ranch just happened to be run by Hans' daughter and son-in-law. It was a large property (for our well-populated county), comprising several hundred acres, all fenced in one pasture. Horses who were boarded at Quail Run ran loose together in a herd, roaming the entire property.

That this was, in some ways, a better way for a horse to live, I couldn't deny. There were, however, some very real disadvantages. It was difficult for an owner to find and/or catch his mount, and the pecking order that evolved in the herd could be brutal for timid horses. But the worst thing, in my opinion, was that Hans' enlightened daughter did no feeding, considering it unnatural. This time of year the grass was sparse and had little feed value, and all the horses out there were pretty damn thin.

"Mary's horse is a Thoroughbred gelding and he's a hard keeper," I said pointedly. "He'll starve."

"He will adjust," Hans rebutted, "and it will be good for him. It is Nature's way. Nature did not intend horses to live in little stalls and pens. You see what comes of it, I told Mary. Such a fire can only occur in a confined situation."

"Right," I said. "I'll send the file over." All I wanted was to get rid of Hans.

"Thank you, my dear." Hans sounded just as courtly and self-satisfied as ever. Nothing seemed to ruffle the man.

I hung up the phone feeling annoyed with the world. First that ass, John, and then Hans. This was really shaping up to be a bad day.

Nancy chose that moment to hand me my list of scheduled calls. Scanning it quickly, I registered mostly familiar names, except the first one.

"Who's that?" I asked, pointing. "A new client?"

"Oh no." Nancy laughed. "She's been with Jim for twenty years."

Well, Nancy ought to know, I thought. *She'd* been with Jim for twenty years.

"I've never seen her, I don't think."

"No. She always uses Jim."

Great, just great. My first call of the day was to a woman who had used no veterinarian other than my boss for twenty years. She would no doubt be thrilled to see me.

I got directions out to Jade Hudson's place and departed. The call sheet said that I would be floating teeth and giving shots to twenty horses, so I made sure I had an adequate number of vaccinations and sedatives in the truck before I pulled out of the office parking lot.

Gritting my teeth, I piloted my way through the heavy early-morning commute traffic, heading for the town of Freedom. Jade Hudson's place was just outside of town.

I found the address without trouble, and turned in to a classic ranch entrance—faded-white-board-fenced pastures lined the long, narrow drive to a house that sat on a little knoll in the center of the property.

The property itself looked fairly extensive—at least a hundred acres, I would guess. The pastures were open and rolling; I could see horses with their heads down, eating flakes of hay, with a backdrop of distant blue hills behind them. It was a pretty sight on a sunny October morning.

The house was large, one-story and plain—an equally classic forties-type ranch house. Like the fences, it looked as if it could use a coat of paint. There was an asphalt parking area in front of it, some scrubby shrubs, and not much in the way of a garden. I got out of my truck and looked around. In another second a woman was walking from the house to greet me.

"Hello. Are you Dr. Gail McCarthy?"

"I am."

"I'm Jade Hudson." We shook hands and sized each other up.

Jade Hudson was in her fifties, by my reckoning. Her long hair, worn in a braid down her back, was an even mix of gray and light brown. Her face, lined by sun and weather, was without makeup, and her faded blue eyes just matched her chambray shirt. She was slim and spare and looked plenty tough, without being in any way harsh. That was what I saw.

I'm not sure exactly what she saw, but after a moment we smiled warmly at each other.

"I'll get a halter," she said.

"All right. What's the program for today?"

"Didn't Jim tell you?"

"He's on vacation."

"That's right." She smiled again. "Do you know anything about what I'm doing here?"

"No, I'm afraid I don't."

Once again, the warm smile. "I retire old horses."

"You do?"

"That's right. Good horses." She glanced at me with a twinkle in her eye. "No outlaws need apply."

"So, all these horses," I gestured at the pasture, "are retirees?"

"Yep."

"Where do they come from?"

"Here and there. I find out about them. They find me."

"I see. What do you do with them?"

"Feed them. Take care of them. Enjoy them."

"Really?" I knew I sounded amazed. "And you pay for all of this yourself?"

"I do." Jade Hudson laughed. "I know. You're thinking I'm both rich and crazy."

"No, not exactly."

"Close, though, right?" We smiled at each other again. "Let me explain," she went on, "just so you won't think you're dealing with a madwoman.

"It all started with Ernie." She pointed at a skinny bay gelding munching alfalfa hay near the fence. "I know he's a little lean," she said, "but he's thirty-seven years old and missing most of his teeth."

"Wow," I said, looking at the horse again. "For thirty-seven, he looks great."

"He's doing well," she said. "He's missing a lot of teeth, like I said, and he has a hard time keeping weight on, but he still feels good. I've had him since I was twenty."

"Wow," I said again. "That's great."

"He's been pretty much retired for the last twenty years, and when I turned him out, I wanted a companion for him. So a friend of mine gave me her old ranch horse to turn out here." She pointed at a black horse next to the bay. "That's Chaw."

"Things just sort of snowballed from there," she went on. "A couple of people came to me and asked me if I'd take their horses. I knew them; they were good people and good horses. So I took them. I made one rule—only gentle geldings. Mares cause trouble, and I didn't want any difficult horses that I couldn't handle.

"Anyway, people heard about me, or I heard about a good horse that needed a home, and, well," she gestured at the herd, "now I've got nineteen of them."

"And you buy their feed?"

"That's right," she said. She looked at me quizzically. "I found I really enjoy retiring these good old guys and giving them a life. It does cost a bit to buy hay for them all, but this is a pretty strong field; I only have to feed once a day, and only in the fall."

She glanced at me. "The truth is, it's become my hobby.

"I don't ride much anymore, but I really love being around horses. I was lucky enough to inherit this place from my parents, and this just seems to me to be a rewarding thing to do with it."

"So you own all this?"

"That's right. Me, myself, and I. Sole proprietor. I had a husband for a while, but he left a dozen years ago. When I turned forty." She gave me a rueful look. "These horses helped me get through it."

"It can be hard."

"It was," she agreed. "But I don't think of him much anymore."

"What do you do?" I asked, genuinely curious.

"You mean, besides look after old horses?" She grinned. "I'm a writer."

"Really? What do you write?"

"Mysteries. Whodunits. I make enough to support myself and my herd."

"That's great." Glancing around, I thought that it sounded in some ways like an idyllic life. Here in her solitary home, Jade Hudson could write her books and enjoy caring for her retirees, free of any encumbrances.

Perhaps mistaking my look for one of appraisal, Jade Hudson said, "I know. It's a little run-down. I don't have enough for frills like paint."

"I wasn't thinking that," I said truthfully. "I was thinking that it seems like a life I'd enjoy."

She looked at me curiously. "Well, most women wouldn't. All my friends think I'm crazy, and wonder why I don't try to find a man. They don't understand that I like my life. I like living alone. I like being free."

"I understand that," I told her. "I've been single all my life and I live alone."

Something in my tone must have caught her attention, because she gave me a discerning look. "Sounds like that's about to change."

"I don't know," I said, sensing that odd intimacy one can

sometimes feel with perfect strangers. "I'm torn."

Jade Hudson, too, seemed to sense our connection. "I know," she said. "I've been there. Several times I almost traded in this life for a man. But somehow, I never quite did."

I nodded. "Me, too. But I feel like I'm getting closer to it."

"Think carefully," she said with a wry look. "My old boys out there give me more pleasure than my husband ever did."

I laughed.

"I'm kidding, of course," she added hastily. "But you know what I mean."

"I do," I agreed. "Horses are great. I could enjoy doing exactly what you do."

Jade Hudson nodded. "Shall we go have a look at them?"

For the next hour I checked teeth and filed them when necessary, gave tetanus shots, and evaluated various soundness problems. Jade knew all of her old boys intimately, and was able to tell me just what sort of problems each had had in the past.

Fortunately all the geldings were easy to catch and handle, and all looked well cared for. Their coats were healthy and their feet were neatly trimmed. As one would expect, many of them were lame.

There were horses with ringbone and horses with sidebone, horses with navicular disease and horses with bone spavin. The list went on and on. All of them were sound enough to get around the pasture, though, and Jade clearly monitored them with care.

"When a horse gets to the end of the road, I put him down," she said. "That's my agreement with the owners. They give the horses to me; all the horses are mine. When I feel their time is up, I make the call."

"How do you decide?" I asked her.

"If I can't keep them at a healthy weight, or they can't move around anymore, or they have too much trouble getting up and down. It's actually pretty obvious."

I nodded. I believed her. You could usually tell when an old animal wasn't enjoying his life any longer.

Jade gestured at the far side of the pasture. "See those seven humps. My neighbor has a backhoe. That's where we bury them."

"I see." I smiled at her. I thought her an entirely likable woman. "Seems like you're doing a good thing."

"I hope so," she said. "I have Jim out once a year, and now," she added, "you. Thanks, Gail."

"Thank you," I said. "I've enjoyed meeting you and your herd. I take it you have an account with us."

"I do," she said. "And thanks again."

I climbed back in my truck and rolled down her driveway wondering quite sincerely if Jade Hudson's wasn't the life I wanted. All this dithering over Blue and Clay was so unrestful, and a relationship, I knew full well from past experience, could be even more so. The tranquillity of the solitary life was in some ways very alluring to me.

Alluring enough?

NINE

Friday night Clay called. I was just climbing into bed after a long week, and I answered the phone reluctantly.

"Gail, Christy George just called here. Her barn's on fire. I know you're not on call, but I thought you'd want to know."

"I'm on my way," I said, as Clay hung up.

Shit. Christy George. The next sizable barn down the road from the Bishop Ranch. It had to be a repeat.

I scrambled into my jeans and sweatshirt, pulled my boots onto bare feet. Even as I dashed from the door to my truck, I registered a breath of warm breeze on my face, heard a soft flickering sound in the big blue gum tree on the ridge.

Oh no, I thought.

My fears were realized as I pulled into Christy George's place fifteen minutes later. Billows of orange flame roiled into the air from the south end of her big barn, fanned by a brisk wind. Already several patches of brush on the hill behind the barn were burning. And the roof of her house was on fire.

"Oh no," I said out loud.

Then I was out of my truck and dashing toward the crowd in front of the barn. People were bringing horses out, I could see, and firefighters were deploying everywhere. Screaming sirens announced the arrival of more.

I didn't see Christy George. I didn't see Clay. I moved toward the barn, trying to decide what I could most usefully do to help.

The knot of spectators around me seemed to surge forward with me; pushing past the man on my right, I registered a familiar face. I did a quick double-take.

Yes, it was him. The same, paunchy, overweight middle-aged man I had shoved past at the Bishop Ranch fire. I recognized his pudgy face, curly hair, heavy glasses. Once again, he stared at the blaze as if mesmerized.

Giving him a long look, I pushed through the people in front of me. "I'm a vet!" I shouted.

The crowd parted slightly; in a minute I'd reached the north entrance to the barn. Christy George came running out, leading a gray horse. Handing his lead rope off to a man, she turned to go back in the barn. I followed her.

Christy grabbed a halter from a rack near the entrance; I did likewise. Then we were running down the central barn aisle toward a roaring inferno at the rear.

I could see people moving through the smoke; someone dashed by, leading a skittering horse. Coughing and choking, holding my breath, I saw Christy disappear into a box stall on my left. Ahead of me a wave of intense heat and light seemed to repel all advance.

A horse neighed on my right. I could see the box stall door. I opened it, and the horse came out almost on top of me.

His wide red chest and the underside of his neck were all I could see; he was tall, towering above me like a giraffe. I slapped his chest as hard as I could and yelled, "Whoa!"

Amazingly, he paused. Even more amazingly he lowered his head and let me put the halter on him. Then we were charging together down the barn aisle, with him more or less dragging me.

Outside the barn, I saw Christy hanging on to a rearing horse.

"Where do you want this one?" I yelled.

"Oh my God. Clifford. Take him down to the ring with the

70

others, I guess. Gail, see if they're all okay." Christy sounded near tears. Then she ran back into the barn.

"Just open all the doors and let them out!" I yelled after her. "We'll catch them out here." I didn't know if she heard me.

Controlling my enormous, skittering charge as well as I could, I led him to the riding ring. A dozen other horses were galloping wildly about inside. Should I let Clifford loose or tie him up?

"We've got some people here to hold horses now." Clay's voice, next to me.

I looked up at him in surprise.

"Give this one to Amy, here, she'll hold him. Let's go catch the rest of them. Christy's afraid they'll hurt themselves. And they're all worth thirty thousand or more." Clay's quiet, competent voice was calming.

Handing Clifford off, I followed Clay into the riding ring. He had an armload of halters and roughly a dozen folks in tow.

"Wait here by the gate," he said to the group at large. "Gail, Tony, and I will catch the horses and bring them up to you. Then just hang onto them and keep them from hurting themselves or each other." Clay's voice stayed calm and confident; his little army arrayed themselves by the gate obediently.

As he distributed halters to myself and Tony Sanchez, a neighboring horseman whom I recognized, Clay's voice was equally controlled. "Let's see if we can get the whole herd cornered down in this end of the arena, away from the fire. See if we can keep them from running. Then we'll walk up to them one-by-one."

Tony and I both nodded and followed Clay. Like a dragnet we pushed the snorting, spooking horses up the riding arena, holding our arms outstretched and stepping sharply in the path of any horse who tried to break and run.

I could hear the roar of the fire behind me and the shouts of the firefighters, but I didn't turn my head to look. Eye contact was important to control the nervous, loose animals. Still, I wondered desperately if the whole hillside was ablaze. Shit. This could be bad.

We had the horse herd cornered now. Wary and scared, the

horses milled nervously in one end of the ring, their eyes on us.

"Tony and I will hold them here," Clay said. "Gail, you catch them one-by-one and bring them to the holders by the gate."

"All right," I said.

Moving slowly, I approached the closest horse—dark, with a white stripe down his face—who looked at me alertly, ears up, muzzle outstretched. As I expected by his expression, he was a pup, standing quietly while I stroked his neck and lowering his nose into the halter willingly.

When I turned to lead him toward the group by the gate, I saw the blaze. "My God," I said.

The barn seemed consumed in flames; they rolled and leaped heavenward. Even as I watched, I could feel waves of heat from the fire, despite the fact that it was several hundred feet away. A steady wind ruffled through my hair. Damn.

The brush on the hill was burning; I could see firefighters at work there, trying to keep the fire controlled. But Christy's house was engulfed; it was an old house with a shake roof, I remembered.

Back to work. Handing my horse off to a holder, I got another halter from Clay and proceeded to capture the next candidate. I evaluated each horse as well as I could. Some coughed; all the rest seemed perfectly fine.

Pointing the coughing horses out to Clay, I said, "I ought to start those on antibiotics."

"Go ahead," he said. "There're only four horses left to catch. Tony and I can handle it."

The little knot of spectators and horse holders was rapidly growing. I hoped that among them would be the horses' owners, or I would find Christy or someone who could give me permission to begin treating the animals.

As I made my way to my truck for supplies, I spotted Hans' silver head in the crowd; he was examining a coughing horse. Sure enough, Hans' truck was parked right next to mine in the drive.

So, where was John, I wondered? Surely one of our clients

would have called in and the answering service had paged him by now; why wasn't he here?

No time to think about it. I got antibiotics and my stethoscope out of the pickup; out of the corner of my eye I registered a sheriff's car pulling in the driveway.

Jeri Ward got out of the car. A man detached himself from a group near a fire engine and walked to meet her. I recognized Walt Harvey.

"Jeri!" I called.

She looked my way. Taking two fast steps toward her, I said, "I've got to run. But there's a man here that I saw at the last fire. His expression is, well, weird. Like he's enjoying it."

"All right," Jeri said. "We're going to be questioning everyone we can. Point this guy out to me."

I scanned the crowd. "There he is." I told her. "Fat guy, near the front of the group staring at the fire. Wearing glasses."

"I've got him," Jeri said.

"He was definitely at the last fire; if he says not, he's lying. I remember him."

"All right."

Jeri and I parted company in a mutual swoop, she toward the crowd by the barn, me toward the riding ring.

I spent the next few hours examining and treating horses. There turned out to be at least a dozen with signs of smoke inhalation problems, and one with fairly severe burns on his neck and rump. At some point in this process, John Romero made an appearance near me.

"Where've you been?" I asked him. "Didn't the service page you?"

"I was out having dinner," he said grudgingly. "It took awhile to get here."

"Jesus, John, I've been here two hours. Where the hell were you?"

"Brookdale. If it's any of your business."

It took me a minute, but I got it. There was only one thing in Brookdale, a little town up in the mountains of the north county, and that was a fairly elaborate restaurant called the Brookdale Lodge. It being Friday night and all, John had probably taken a lady friend to dinner. No wonder he was even more surly than usual.

"It should only have taken an hour to get here," I said.

John shrugged.

Infuriated at his attitude, I turned away and moved on to the next horse without a word. This was all getting to be too damned much.

Another hour later, all horses had been examined and treated, and the inferno seemed to be subsiding. Despite the wind, the firefighters had managed to control the brush fire. But the barn and house were a total loss.

I saw Christy standing near a horse, and walked up to her.

"Oh, Gail, thank you." Christy sounded as if she were crying.

I put a hand on her arm. "I'm sorry," I said. "What a mess."

"I know. But at least we only lost one horse." Christy gulped and went on. "And you got Clifford out. I can't believe he was still in there. I thought someone told me they'd already gotten him out."

"Clifford?"

"The horse you got out of the barn. That's Clifford. He's the most valuable horse out here."

"Oh." I remembered Clifford now. So many things had happened since I rescued him, I'd forgotten all about it.

Christy shook her head. "The woman who owns him paid over eighty thousand for him."

"Wow."

"Yeah." Christy gave me a weak smile. "He's got a fancy German name I can't pronounce. Clifford's just his barn name."

I must have looked puzzled.

Christy cocked her head. "You know, Clifford the big, red dog. Clifford the horse is just a big, sweet pup."

I shook my head, not understanding the allusion.

"It's a kids' book," Christy said, and burst into sobs.

I put an awkward arm around her shoulders as she cried.

"All my daughter's books were in that house. And all her baby

74

pictures," Christy gasped out. "They're all gone. And she's grown up now; I don't have anything left from when she was a baby."

"Did you get all your pets out?" I asked gently.

"Yeah. I shut the dogs in the pickup; it's parked way out there." Christy waved an arm at the drive. "I don't know about the cats. They were barn cats. I hope they got out. I haven't seen them."

"I'm sorry," I said again, feeling how inadequate it was.

As I spoke, a woman detached herself from the crowd and threw her arms around Christy. The two of them wept on each other's shoulders. I watched them sympathetically, not knowing what to say or do.

Christy George was about my own age. I'd known her to be divorced and single, living alone here and running a boarding stable that catered to high-priced dressage horses. I hadn't known she had a daughter.

Christy's operation was much smaller than the Bishop Ranch; I thought she had about twenty horses on her place, total. But all of them were worth a lot of money, and Christy charged high rates and gave her boarders deluxe care. I couldn't imagine how she was going to cope with such a large-scale disaster.

I felt a tap on my arm. "Gail?"

It was Clay. "Hey," I said.

"I'm going home now," he told me. "Mom's not feeling well and she's alone. I need to get back. Just thought I'd let you know."

"Thanks," I said. And then, "Where's Bart?"

"Out on a date. That's what Mom said. I'd guess with Angie."

"Oh." Belatedly I realized I hadn't seen Bart tonight. "Well, thanks for letting me know about this. I'm glad I could be here to help."

"Yeah. I was glad you were here, too." Clay squeezed my hand briefly and turned away.

Other people were departing, too, I noticed. Maybe I could go. Christy George was talking to the woman who had hugged her. My junior vet and supposed cohort was nowhere to be seen.

Hans Schmidt was gone, too. I wondered what time it was.

Scanning what was left of the crowd, I saw Jeri Ward talking to a teenage boy over by her sedan. I walked in their direction.

The boy was tall and thin with pale skin, wearing a ball cap and denim jacket. His eyes moved restlessly as he spoke to Jeri. There was something defiant in his stance; at the same time he looked uncomfortable.

As I approached, Jeri glanced my way and then said something that appeared to be conclusive. The boy answered her, then slouched away.

I watched his loose-hipped, slump-shouldered shuffle, and asked Jeri, "Who's that?"

"That," she said, "is Marty Martin. That's what he calls himself. Suspect number one, at the moment."

"Ah," I said. "I thought suspect number one was Bart Bishop."

"He's been replaced. Marty, there, is actually Bart's pick for chief suspect."

"Oh, yeah," I said. "Bart told me."

"So, of course, I checked him out. Turns out we're very familiar with Marty Martin."

"Familiar?"

"He's got one of the longest rap sheets for a juvenile I've ever seen."

"Oh."

"Yeah. Marty's been arrested for everything from petty theft to possession of pot, to guess what? Arson."

"Oh," I said again.

"Yeah," Jeri said again. "He burned the neighbor's shed down when he got mad at her. Told her she'd be sorry when she ran him off her place, which is what he allegedly said to Bart Bishop. Quite the coincidence."

"So, how come he's running around loose?"

"Marty's father has a lot of money," Jeri said succinctly.

It figured. Everyone who lived in Lushmeadows subdivision had a fair amount of money.

"Also," Jeri said, "Marty committed those crimes as a juvenile. But this time it'll be different."

"Why's that?"

Jeri smiled. "Marty turned eighteen last month."

TEN

At ten the next morning I was down at my barn, waiting for Blue Winter. We'd agreed on this time for my initial training session with Danny, and I was keen to begin. Sitting on a bale in the hay barn, I rubbed Roey's red, wedge-shaped head and stared impatiently down my driveway, much as I had as a five-year-old, waiting for my father.

Danny stood in his corral, munching the last of his breakfast hay and eyeing me curiously. Despite my eagerness to begin, I refrained from grabbing a halter and catching the colt. I wanted Blue with me, as an observer and an advisor. Though I was familiar with equine ways in general, I was aware of my ignorance about the breaking process. I'd read some books, sure; I'd seen people get on colts for the first time. But neither of these was an excuse for real hands-on experience. Which Blue had.

Why, I wondered suddenly, had I never told Clay about my new project? The answer came to me just as quickly. Because of Bart. Bart was a horse trainer by profession, and Clay would probably have suggested that his brother help me with the colt. And I was not a great fan of Brother Bart. In my opinion, Bart's attitude was egotistical and his method rigid; neither was an advantage in a horse trainer.

Still, I was glad to hear he was off the hook as chief arson suspect. I hadn't really believed he'd burn his own barn down, and I felt the distress the whole situation seemed to be causing Clay.

Was Marty Martin the culprit? Jeri seemed to think so, but I wondered. I couldn't forget the expression on the fat man's face as he stared at the blaze.

Once again, I shifted my attention to the drive. Where was Blue?

High on the eastern ridge, the big blue gum whispered softly. Morning sunlight seemed almost to glitter on the smooth lance-shaped leaves. Each plumey bough was mounded with a load of little silvery blue cones, like some sort of magically moonlit snow. Slender, branching trunks reached skyward, creaking and swaying in the breeze, towering high above the ridge and my property.

I smiled. Eucalyptus trees are notorious for coming down in a storm. But my big tree was far enough away from my house and barn not to be a hazard, and I loved it. It was the only really big tree on my property, and as such had a special presence for me. My bedroom window looked out at it; I had seen it glowing in the light of the full moon and silhouetted against the dawn. Were I to make a shrine, it would be at the base of that tree.

Still no sign of Blue. I scanned the sky impatiently. Though the air was warm and dry, little feathery clouds scudded along, drawn by the breeze. Perhaps the weather was changing.

At last. And at last, too, the shape of a dark green pickup could be seen pulling in my front gate. Blue was here.

I waited quietly on my hay bale as Blue parked and got out of his truck. My heart seemed to move, literally, as he turned, saw me, and smiled.

What is it, I asked myself, not for the first time, about this man?

He walked toward me, red hair shining like fine, coppery gold wires in a springy halo beneath his gray fedora hat, and all I wanted to do was fall into those long arms like some kind of storybook maiden and have him hold me.

79

Our eyes met. Blue smiled again; I wondered what he was thinking.

"Morning, Stormy," he said. "I'm sorry I'm late. One of my guys quit this morning and I had to scramble around to find some help. Little plants take a lot of looking after in this heat."

"I can imagine. Looks like the weather might be breaking," I added.

Blue glanced skyward. "It does," he agreed. "That wind last night made me think a front might be coming in."

"Yeah," I said. "Another barn in Harkins Valley burned last night."

"Oh no," Blue said. "Arson?"

"Everyone seems to think so. It was Christy George's place. Do you know her?"

"I don't believe so."

"She runs a fancy dressage stable. She's a single woman; the boarding stable is her livelihood. I'm afraid this will be really hard on her. Her house burned to the ground, too. I sure hope she has good insurance."

"Wow." Blue shook his head. "So the cops think some arsonist is getting his kicks burning horse barns down."

"Apparently. They seem to think it's a neighbor kid who's been in a lot of trouble." I shrugged. "I guess we'll see."

"You're friends with that detective, right?"

"Jeri Ward. Yeah, we're friends. Or almost friends, anyway. We've known each other awhile." Picking Danny's halter up from the bale beside me, I said, "Are you ready?"

"Sure."

Danny walked to meet me, ears up, as I opened his corral gate. So, what interesting thing are we going to do, his bright-eyed expression asked.

I led the colt up to my round pen, Blue walking along beside us. Once we were in the pen, I turned Danny loose. The horse walked a few steps and then broke into a trot of his own accord. Blue and I stood in the center of the pen and watched him trot around us.

"He's a nice mover," Blue said quietly.

"Yeah. I thought so, too. So, tell me what you see."

Blue thought a minute, his eyes on Danny. "He's a calm, sensible colt," he said at last. "He looks easygoing to me. And he's got that long, flat stride, uses his hind leg real well. I like him. What's been done with him so far?"

"Glen said he's been handled some, not a lot. Enough to be halter broke and to be comfortable having his feet trimmed, being wormed, the usual stuff. Mostly he's just been running around a forty-acre pasture with a couple of other colts."

"And he's how old?"

"Three."

"Sounds just right to me," Blue said. "Generally speaking, colts are easier to work with if they haven't been messed with too much, and it looks like he has a naturally gentle disposition, just watching the way he behaves."

"So, what should I do?" I asked him.

Blue watched the horse. Danny came to a stop and looked in our direction. "Let him come to you and pet him," Blue said.

I held my hand out.

Easily, as if he'd done it a hundred times, Danny walked up to me. I rubbed his forehead.

Blue smiled. "He'll be a piece of cake," he said. Then he looked at me. "So, what's your plan here?"

"Work him in the round pen a little. Maybe saddle him. What do you think?"

"I think," he said slowly, "that sounds fine. Tom always taught me to move along with the breaking just as fast or as slow as a colt wants to go. They're all different. If a colt didn't show any fear at all, we'd sometimes work him in the pen, and saddle him and ride him, all in the first session. Other times, when a colt would stick at some part of the process, like the saddling, and seem afraid of it, we'd do nothing but work with him a little bit every day until he wasn't afraid of the saddle anymore. We might not get on him for a month.

"I'd say the main thing is just to get him working well in the pen and paying attention to you, and then see how far he wants to go with the breaking process. He'll let you know."

81

"Okay," I said, rubbing Danny's face. "Keep giving me your input."

For the next half hour, I worked the colt in the pen, teaching him to trot and then lope around me in both directions, stop when I said whoa, and come to me to be petted when I held my hand up. Danny learned these things quickly, without showing any fear or resentment. He seemed to take it all as a game and be perfectly willing to play.

Blue confirmed my impression. "He's enjoying this," he said. "I think you could move on to the saddling now, if you wanted. The trick with these real smart horses who want to learn is to move right along. They get bored if you dink around doing the same thing over and over."

Walking to the gate, I fetched my saddle and a couple of pads from the spot where I'd stashed them.

"So, do I sack him out with one of these pads?"

Blue shrugged. "If it were me, I'd just put the pad on him and see how he feels about it."

I flipped the saddle pad up on Danny's back; he barely twitched.

Blue smiled. "The thing is, some people want to fan these horses all over with saddle blankets and do all these sacking procedures, and maybe a given individual doesn't need that. He doesn't mind the saddle pad on his back. Now, if he would have shown any fear of it, I would have suggested you work with him a little."

"What about the saddle?" I asked.

"Let him look at it first. Let's see what he thinks. Always take your cue from the horse," he added. "That's the main thing Tom taught me."

I carried the saddle up to Danny and set it on the ground in front of him. He put his head down and sniffed the leather. Lifting his head, he snorted softly, then sniffed the saddle again. Then he bumped it with his nose.

Picking the saddle up, I held it next to his shoulder. Danny reached back and sniffed again. I swung the stirrups so they creaked, slapped the cinch up and down, shook the whole rig a little. Danny seemed profoundly unimpressed. He cocked one ear at me as if to say, What's next?

"Set it on his back," Blue said. "Be ready to lift it off if he seems afraid."

I swung the saddle gently onto Danny's back. For a second his eyes widened, then he stretched his muzzle back to sniff a stirrup, seemed to recognize it as familiar, and relaxed.

Blue grinned. "Lift it off and put it on him again," he said.

I swung the saddle on and lifted it off half a dozen times. The last time I did it, Danny cocked a hip and stood with his weight off one hind foot, in a horse's classic resting pose.

"Looks pretty relaxed to me," Blue said.

"So, what now?" I asked.

"You could quit. He's done well, learned a lot. Or you could try cinching him."

"What would you do?"

"Cinch him. Nothing you've done so far has even ruffled his feathers."

"All right."

I lowered the cinch off the right-hand side of the saddle. After rubbing Danny's belly a few times, I drew the cinch underneath him and ran the latigo through the buckle. Working quietly, I pulled the cinch until it was gently snug, not so tight that it would be uncomfortable, not so loose that the saddle could slip under the horse's belly. Then I stepped back.

Danny just looked at me.

"Ask him to move," Blue said.

I clucked to the colt. He took a step forward and his head came up as he felt the unfamiliar pressure around his heartgirth. Breaking into a trot, he moved around the pen, snorting and scooting forward when the swinging stirrups touched his sides. Blue and I watched him closely.

Danny's eyes showed mild concern. Not alarm, nothing close to panic. He kept trotting, every once in a while jumping ahead when the feel of the saddle surprised him. After a few minutes, he started to flatten out. His eye grew calmer. In another minute he began making chewing motions with his mouth and his trot slowed.

Blue pointed. "See that mouthing he's doing?"

"Uh-huh."

"That's a sign of acceptance. Actually, it's a sign of submission. When a horse makes that gesture, it means he's accepted what you're doing, or learned whatever lesson you're trying to teach him. It's the same signal baby colts give when they're relating to an adult horse. It means, 'You're dominant.' "

I held my hand up and Danny coasted to a stop in front of me. I rubbed his forehead and he sighed.

"Enough for today?" I asked Blue.

"You bet. He's learned a bunch. If he goes as well as this, I think you could ride him next session."

"Really?"

"If you want. Of course, that's up to you."

"I'm willing."

I unsaddled Danny, being careful not to scare him, and led him down to his corral and put him away.

"Ready for a sandwich and a beer?" I asked Blue.

"You bet," he said.

We walked side-by-side up to my house, Roey trotting at our heels. I couldn't help but think how wonderfully companionable it all was. What would it be like to have a partner like this, someone with whom I could share my life?

I fixed Blue a sandwich and brought him a beer. When he was done, he stood up.

"Unfortunately, I need to go back and check on my young plants. They're at a touchy stage right now and this heat is worrying me." He hesitated. "Would you like to come over to dinner tonight?"

My turn to hesitate, as I tried to recall if I had any other commitments.

Misunderstanding my silence, Blue said sheepishly, "I'm not the world's greatest cook."

"No, no," I said quickly. "I'd love to come. I think I'm free and clear. I'm not even on call." Inwardly my heart was singing.

"Five o'clock all right?"

"I'll be there," I told him.

He started for the door and then looked back.

"Do you like paella?" he asked.

Paella? What the hell is paella, I wondered. I smiled at him. "I love it," I said.

ELEVEN

I drove in the entrance of Brewer's Rose Farm at five-fifteen, a time I'd carefully calculated. Not so late as to be rude, late enough that Blue would be waiting for me. I passed the office, the display gardens, the greenhouses. Blue lived "out back"— behind the facility. I'd been to his place once before.

Parking my truck next to his in the drive, I got out with a smile on my face. Blue's dwelling was every bit as unique as my own.

Perched on a bluff overlooking rolling agricultural fields that swept down to the Monterey Bay, Blue's little travel trailer was sheltered by a simple pole barn with a tin roof. In front was a veranda, and climbing roses had been trained up the posts and along the roof. The vines were turning golden now and they were covered with tiny glowing red rosehips, like fairy lanterns. Two wooden chairs and a table underneath the arbor faced south-west—out to sea.

A couple of short, sharp barks alerted me to the presence of Freckles, Blue's little dog. She came dashing out from under the trailer, waving her white plume of a tail, her spotted form wiggling in greeting. I rubbed her head and let her sniff my hand and she trotted happily along beside me.

As I made my way to the door, I glanced with surprise at the corrals behind Blue's trailer.

"Where are the horses?" I asked, as he opened his door.

Blue didn't say anything. Stepping back, he gestured that I should come in.

A wave of rich scent rolled over me as I walked into the trailer, Freckles at my heels. Aromatic and rich—spices and onions and olive oil and what?

"Wow," I said. "Whatever you're cooking smells wonderful."

"Paella," Blue said briefly, and went to stir the contents of the skillet. "How about a margarita?" he asked, with his back to me.

"Sure." I settled myself in the one armchair in Blue's living room. Even tinier than my own living-room area, the room had a cozy feel, like the cabin of a boat. The walls were paneled with warm, teak-colored wood and there were windows on all sides. A small couch, the chair, and a desk filled the available space.

Blue busied himself making margaritas in the kitchen. I stroked the arm of the chair I was sitting in. Like the desk, the chair was somewhat Victorian, with curving, carved wooden arms and legs. It was upholstered in a soft moss green velvet and seemed to curl itself comfortably around me. A lamp placed just next to it and a stack of books alongside indicated its primary use.

Freckles lay down at my feet and put her nose on her paws. Giving a long sigh, she settled her body against my ankles, as if it were an accustomed routine.

I gazed around the little room and smiled.

"So, you don't have a TV?" I asked Blue.

"No." He shrugged, his back still to me. "I like to read." He waved one hand at the computer on the desk. "I can watch videos on the monitor if I want."

"Sounds good to me. I haven't lived with a TV since I've been able to own my own place."

Blue said nothing.

I hesitated, then asked again, "Are the horses gone?"

Blue kept making margaritas and didn't reply.

I considered. Should I ask again, as if I believed he hadn't heard me? He had heard me though; I was sure of it. Should I just shut up about the horses and assume he didn't want to tell me what had happened to them?

I thought about that. Then I said, "Do you not want to talk about it?"

Blue turned toward me, holding two short glasses filled with ice cubes and lemon-lime-colored drink. Handing me one of the glasses, he touched the other to it with a slight clink.

"Here's to you, Stormy," he said. And then, after a quick swallow, he met my eyes. "It's not that I don't want to tell you, it's just that I'm not sure what to say."

I waited.

"I sold Dunny to a friend," he said at last, "and leased the mare to another friend who wants to raise babies out of her. They both went to good homes."

"But, why?" I asked in surprise.

Blue looked down and took another swallow of his drink. "I have to move," he said at last, "and I didn't think I'd be able to take them."

"You have to move?"

"Yeah. We're expanding the greenhouse range." Blue gave me a quick smile. "Our growing operation is doing really well. But the only place for the new greenhouse is right here. So, I have to move."

"Where will you go?"

"I don't know yet. The Brewers have given me a big raise to compensate for losing my living space, and the trailer's mine, so I can move it somewhere else, but I've looked into it, and the only option I can afford would be a trailer park."

I winced.

"Things are pretty expensive in Santa Cruz County," Blue went on. "I had hoped I could buy a piece of land, but it seems impossible. Even finding a spot in a trailer park is looking problematic. I'll probably have to sell the trailer and just rent an apartment in Watsonville. So you can see why I had to get rid of the horses."

"That must have been hard," I said sympathetically.

"Not so much," Blue said. "They both went to good homes, like I said. I can see them and know they're doing fine. It's okay."

"But how can you stand to move from here to an apartment in Watsonville?"

Blue got up and stirred his skillet. "I can stand a lot of things," he said quietly, with his back to me.

I took a swallow of my drink and watched his broad back under the blue denim shirt.

"So, what's paella?" I asked him.

"It's a rice dish made with saffron. It usually has some kind of seafood, maybe sausage, maybe chicken. It varies according to locale. I learned my version in the South of France. In my misspent youth."

"Did you have a misspent youth?"

"Depends what you mean." Blue turned and smiled at me. "I think my folks hoped I'd go to college, become a doctor or a lawyer or an engineer. The American dream and all that.

"When I got out of high school I told my dad I wanted to travel. He said it was probably a good thing for a young man to see a bit of the world in the year between high school and college. So off I went."

Blue smiled at me again. "I didn't come back for ten years."

"Did you support yourself the whole time?"

"I did. My father wasn't a rich man, and I wouldn't have asked him for money, anyway. I'd saved all the money I made working for Tom Billings; that's what got me started. And then I just worked my way along.

"I was a dishwasher in France, and I worked for a greenhouse grower one winter in Greece while I waited for the weather to turn warm so I could go to India. I was a gardener in Australia. I taught English in Iran." Blue grinned. "They fired me because I couldn't spell. In between jobs, I smuggled a little pot to make ends meet."

"You sold pot?" I was quite honestly surprised.

"I told you I had a misspent youth." Blue shrugged. "I spent time in jail in Bali, too."

"You did?" Jail in Bali sounded a good deal more exotic than most personal histories I'd listened to. "What were you in jail for?"

"Possession of marijuana." Blue shrugged again. "I was there six months. Had to bribe my way out."

"And then you were taught by the senior tutor of the Dalai Lama?"

"That's right. Quite the study in contrasts, my life."

"It is that." I took another swallow of my drink and stared at Blue in fascination as he stirred his skillet. I had never met anyone remotely like him before. "What other adventures have you had?"

"Well, I hiked through parts of India that probably hadn't seen a white man since the Raj. Little children would run and hide behind their mothers when they saw me. They thought I was a devil. If I stopped at a tea shop, a crowd would gather, as if I were some exotic animal exhibit."

"Wow." I laughed.

"Yeah." Blue poured a little more margarita into both our glasses. "I ended up going trekking in the Himalayas and got lost one night in a snowstorm. It got so dark I couldn't see and the terrain was so treacherous that I was afraid to move around at all, even to make camp. I thought I'd fall into a ravine. I had no wood to make a fire, so I just stood next to a big rock that sheltered me some and pretty much ran in place all night to keep from freezing to death. It was a long night, I can tell you."

"Wow," I said again.

Blue laughed. "That wasn't the worst of it. Somehow during that trip I ended up catching hepatitis, and I was so sick when I made it back to Kathmandu I could barely walk. I managed to get on an airplane and fly to Bangkok, where there were doctors, and I lived there in the Hotel Malaysia for six weeks—basically living off room service."

"All alone?" I asked.

"All alone," he said. "That did get me down. I almost flew

back to the States when I felt a little better. But somehow, I didn't. I went to Australia instead."

"Wow," I said yet again.

"So, you see," Blue smiled at me, "moving to an apartment in Watsonville is not really a big deal."

"I see," I said. This man had certainly been through enough to be able to put life's ups and downs in proportion.

Taking another sip of my drink, I asked him, "You spent quite a bit of time in Australia, didn't you?"

"Five years," he said.

"And then you came back to America?"

"Not exactly. I traveled around the East for a while before I came home."

"I bet you had a few more adventures," I teased him.

"Am I boring you?" Blue gave me an inquiring look.

"Not at all. Really. Truly. I'm fascinated."

Blue began ladling food onto plates. Over his shoulder, he said, "I did have a few more interesting experiences. I left Australia as part of a crew on a boat that was solely powered by wind. No engine at all. We were on our way to a remote Indonesian island to pick up another sailboat. On the way we got becalmed, and a trip that was supposed to take three days took three weeks."

"What did you do?"

"Fortunately, we were prepared. We had enough water, and the hold was full of a kind of pumpkin they called a 'Queensland Blue.' And we fished, of course. We had pumpkin soup and fried pumpkin, and innumerable versions of fish-and-pumpkin stew." Blue grinned. "To this day I don't care if I ever eat any kind of squash again."

I laughed.

Blue handed me a plate of fragrant, steaming rice and seafood. "It's sort of a one-dish meal, I'm afraid," he said.

I accepted a fork, napkin, and a glass of white wine and told him truthfully, "It's perfect. Just the sort of meal I like."

Paella turned out to be wonderful. The saffron added a subtle flavor, warm and rich, not peppery. Blue's dish included clams, shrimp, chicken, and bell peppers. "The way I learned to make it in the Pyrenees," he said.

"You've certainly led an interesting life."

"That's one way of putting it. I'm afraid my parents might be more inclined to go with the misspent-youth theory."

"Why did you come back to America?" I asked him.

"My parents," he said simply. "I'm their only living child and they're getting older. I felt I needed to live where I could see them from time to time."

"But you didn't move back to the family farm."

"No, by the time I came back, they'd sold the farm and moved into the condo in Fresno. But I would never have chosen to live in the Central Valley, anyway. Too claustrophobic for me. I always knew that if I came back to the States to live, it would be on the California coast."

"And here you are."

"And here I am," he agreed. "Close enough to visit my folks two or three times a year, and living in one of the most beautiful places on earth."

"You ought to know," I said.

Blue smiled.

"How'd you end up working at the rose farm?"

He shrugged one shoulder. "I knew I wanted a job in agriculture, and I liked the Monterey Bay area. So I went around to various greenhouse growers and asked for work. Brewer's needed a laborer."

"You started at the bottom, then?"

"Oh yeah. I started out watering plants for minimum wage."

"And went on to become their breeder and greenhouse manager."

Blue shrugged again and looked down. I stared at him. The curling red-gold hair, the long, lean, muscular frame, the slender hands and strong chin. I ached to touch him. I took a swallow of wine and went back to eating paella.

Blue looked up from his food. "Are we going to work with your colt tomorrow?"

"If you have time, I'd love to have you there. Do you really think I ought to ride him?"

"It depends. If you go through the same routine you did today, and he doesn't show any fear, I'd get on him, sure."

"We haven't even bridled him yet."

Blue drank some wine and said slowly, "The way Tom taught me, we got on them before we bridled them. We always rode them for the first time with the halter on their heads, and we did it as soon as they were comfortable with a saddle on their backs. Like I said, for some horses that takes quite awhile. Others, like your Danny, get there very quickly."

"Why do you get on them like that?" I asked him.

"It's easier for them. We didn't try to control them much, just got them to move around, get used to having a human on their backs. When they were used to that, which usually takes somewhere between three and a dozen rides, depending on the horse, we'd start putting the bridle on them and teach them to be guided by the reins."

"So what happens," I said carefully, "if you get on one with just a halter on him and he decides he wants to buck?"

Blue smiled at me. "A relevant question, from your point of view."

"That's right." I laughed.

"Well, first off, a colt will buck you off with a bridle on his head just as well as he will with a halter, if that's what he wants to do. A bit won't stop a green horse from bucking, nor will he usually respond to it much. Having a bit in his mouth is more likely just to scare a colt. So, a bridle's no protection.

"What I've found is, if you get on a colt and just stay relaxed, let him move however he wants to move, hold onto the saddle horn if you need to, just pretend you're a sack of potatoes, they mostly never buck. If they do, you just encourage them to move forward with your legs, and most of the time, they'll come out of it." Blue looked at me. "I'll ride your colt for you, if you'd like me to."

I shook my head. "No. That's the point. I want the experience of breaking a horse. I want to be the first one on him. But I'm curious about one thing. Is there any reason to be in a hurry about it?"

Blue sighed. "Well, there is and there isn't. No, you don't need to hurry, but you do get a feel for these things. I'd say your colt was ready to ride. If you put it off because you're afraid of him, well, I don't know how to say this, but the horse will know. If you just get on him and ride him like it's no big deal, it will be no big deal.

"If you hold off and dink around and dink around, bridling him and sacking him and checking him up and tying him around and driving him, like I've seen people do, all because you're essentially afraid to get on him, the horse senses that getting on him is a big deal to you. So it becomes a big deal to him."

"I see," I said. "They do seem to sense what we're feeling, don't they?"

"They do," Blue agreed. He smiled at me. "How about you? Do you sense what I'm feeling?"

I wrinkled my nose at him. "Would it involve me sitting next to you?"

"It would," he said. Putting the crockery aside on the counter, he patted the couch next to him.

I smiled and got up and settled myself into the curve of his body. Putting my hands on either side of his face, I pulled his mouth gently down toward mine. "Did you know I've been wanting to do this all night?" I asked him.

"I know I wanted to," he murmured.

Then we were quiet, kissing, touching, exploring. I stroked Blue's back; he ran his fingers through my hair and unbuttoned my blouse. Delicately, shyly, he unbuttoned his own shirt and then pressed the bare skin of his chest against mine.

We held each other like that for a long time, nuzzling and kissing. As I fitted my mouth to his, I was aware of a subtle, elusive sweetness in the air, a scent that seemed to drift through the open windows and mingle with the smell of the sea.

"What's the perfume I smell?" I said softly into Blue's hair. "It smells like flowers, but your roses aren't in bloom."

"I've got a tub of jasmine and nicotiana planted outside my bedroom window," he said. "I like the way it smells when I go to bed. Maybe you might like it, too."

I ran my fingers through the curls at the back of his neck and down his spine. I felt light-headed with desire.

"Maybe I'll just have to see," I said.

Blue stood up and held out his hand.

For a second I hesitated, my mind shouting its innumerable warnings. But the rush of sweet pleasure in my body mingling with the heady sweetness in the air was too strong. It drew me toward Blue; I stood and put my hand in his. He kissed me gently and led me into the bedroom.

Like the living room, Blue's bedroom was tiny, paneled in teak like the cabin of a boat. The double bed was covered with a Navajo blanket in sandstone red, sage green, sky blue. The windows by the bed were uncurtained and open. I could smell the scent of flowers.

Quietly, Blue slipped my blouse off my shoulders and stroked my back with his hands. Reaching up, I put my arms around him and buried my face in his skin, in the unique, personal odor of him.

"I want you, Gail," he said. "I'll do my best to be good to you." He bent down and I could feel his mouth moving down my neck and my breasts.

I sighed. Every atom in my body felt as if it were rushing to meet his.

"I think I'm ready," I told him, as I put my hand on his belt buckle.

TWELVE

I woke up Sunday morning in Blue's bed. Waking in a new lover's bed can be disconcerting or delightful. In this case, it was the latter.

I opened my eyes to Blue's mouth on mine, and then, gently, he moved on. He kissed my body leisurely and at length. I watched him in the mirror that hung on his closet.

We were a pretty sight, naked and intertwined in the early-morning light. His long, muscled arms round my curves, his red-gold hair tangling with my dark curls. Like some ancient Greek sculpture, I thought. And then I didn't think anymore.

An hour or so later, I woke again, this time from a satiated doze. Blue lay with his head propped on one elbow, looking down at me.

Feeling suddenly shy, I pulled the sheet up over my body.

"No, no," he said quietly. "You're beautiful. I was just think-ing that you here in my bed is one of the most beautiful sights I've ever seen."

I blushed. I could feel the tide of color in my cheeks.

Blue smiled. "How about some coffee?"

"That would be great."

He climbed out of bed and I admired every inch of his long,

lean, naked body as he moved across the room. Come what may, I thought, this is a delicious moment.

Five minutes later, Blue was back with freshly brewed coffee in two mugs with dragons on them. Cream and sugar waited in matching containers; the whole thing was arranged on a lacquered wood tray. Blue set the little tray on the bed next to me and picked up one of the cups.

"Good morning, Stormy," he said.

"Good morning." I smiled at him. "It's been a good morning so far."

"It has at that." Blue grinned back. "So what's next on the agenda?"

"Well, much as I'd like to roll around in bed all day, I suppose I ought to go home and feed my animals."

"All right." Blue ran one hand down my bare leg. "Can I make you breakfast first?"

"You can." I smiled at him again, liking everything about him. I hadn't exactly thought out my decision to go to bed with him last night, but maybe it was going to turn out all right, anyway. What the hell, I told myself, as I sipped hot coffee and admired Blue's body in the morning light. I was ready to give this a try.

Blue made me an omelet for breakfast; there was fresh-squeezed orange juice to go with it.

"Do you always eat this well?" I asked him.

He smiled shyly at me. "I was kind of hoping you'd stay," he said.

I put my hand in his. "I'm glad I did," I said. "But I'd better go. My horses and my dog are waiting for me."

"I need to go check around my greenhouse," Blue said. "Shall I be out at your place in, say, a couple of hours?"

"That would be great," I said.

Two hours later I was once again sitting on a bale in my barn, waiting for Blue. A good deal less impatiently than I had the day before. My whole body felt relaxed and content. I stroked Roey's head and enjoyed my tranquillity.

"I needed that," I told the dog.

And then Blue was driving up my driveway. He parked his truck and got out, just as he had before, but this time, when he walked to meet me, he reached for my hand, pulled me to him, and kissed me long and lingeringly on the mouth.

"I missed you," he said.

"In two hours," I teased.

"I'm just like an eighteen-year-old with his first lover," Blue agreed. "I can't wait to see you."

I laughed. "You make me feel good."

"Are you ready to ride Dannyboy?"

"You bet."

Together we caught the colt and took him to the round pen, Roey trotting behind us.

"You didn't bring Freckles?" I asked him.

"I thought you might not want her out at your place."

"She got along fine with Roey on the pack trip last summer. Let's give it a try next time."

"All right, I'll bring her," Blue said.

I led Danny into the round pen and turned him loose. Once again he broke into a frisky little trot and coasted around me for a lap or two, then slowed to a walk. After a minute he stopped and looked at me.

Raising my hand, I met his eyes. Instantly, he walked to meet me. I rubbed his dark red forehead and straightened the black forelock.

"What now?" I asked Blue.

"I'd go through everything you did yesterday, but move along a little quicker if he seems to remember and accept each step. Then, we'll see."

"Okay," I said.

I put Danny through his paces; he seemed relaxed and confident, showing no fear of the saddle blanket or the saddle. He moved calmly with the saddle on his back and responded to my cues to trot and lope with it. Finally I told him whoa and raised my hand.

After our ritual head rub, I said to Blue, "So, now do I just get on him?" My heart was pounding.

Blue regarded me. "Gail, I don't want you to feel I'm pressuring you into something you don't want to do."

"No," I said. "I can feel that he's ready, just like you said. It's time. I am a little nervous about it, though."

"I used to get scared, when I first started getting on colts," Blue said. "Tom told me a few things that really helped me." He looked at me inquiringly.

"Fire away," I said. "Believe me, I'm listening."

"First of all," Blue said, "I found it helps to acknowledge what is. If you feel fear, let yourself acknowledge and accept those feelings. Don't push them away. A lot of people find fear very uncomfortable so they try to pretend they're not feeling it. I think that just causes the fear to hide in their bodies, makes them tense.

"So what I learned to do was to take a deep breath and then let it out real slow. I would try to feel the fear, wherever it was in my body—the tightness in my thighs, the butterflies in my stomach, whatever. I'd say to myself, I'm feeling some fear, here. That's okay. Then I'd take another deep breath and let it out and try to let go of as much tension as I could."

"Okay," I said, taking a deep breath. "I can feel the tension in my legs."

"That's right," Blue said. "Let it be there. Let it be okay. Then take another deep breath and let go of it as much as you can; consciously relax. And try to keep your mind on what's happening now.

"The thing about fear is that it's mostly about something that might happen, not about something that is happening. Fear tends to center around 'what if?' So, if you keep your mind in the present, if you stay with what's happening now, fear gets less of a grip on you."

I thought about it. "That's true," I said. "Any other advice?"

"Talk to him the whole time."

"All right," I said. "Here goes."

Checking Danny's cinch to make sure it was snug enough, I took a deep breath and let it out slowly, trying to release the tightness in my muscles. I could feel my heart pounding. It's okay, I told myself. It's okay to be scared and all that is happening now is I am putting my foot in the stirrup. Danny is standing quietly. Nothing else.

"I'm putting my foot in the stirrup," I said out loud to the colt. "Now I'm putting my weight in the stirrup."

I stood in the left stirrup and Danny looked back at me, mildly puzzled, but calm.

"I'm swinging my leg over your back," I told him. "Now I'm sitting on your back." I reached down and stroked his neck. "I'm riding you."

Danny bent his neck so he could reach back and sniff my boot in the stirrup. He still stood quietly.

"What now?" I said to Blue.

"Ask him to take a step. Use your heels to bump him and the halter rope to guide him."

Gently, I pulled Danny's nose to the left with the lead rope and bumped my heels against his sides. He took a step, then another. I clucked to him and steered him with the rope and he walked around the ring, a little uncertainly and awkwardly, but completely docile.

"My God," I said to Blue. "That was easy."

"Step one," he said.

"I know, I've got a long way to go. But I did it. We did it." I patted Danny's neck again, my heart still pounding, but with exhilaration more than fear.

I walked the colt around for a few more minutes, then dismounted and mounted again. After I'd mounted him a half dozen times, Blue suggested I quit for the day.

"He's done real well," he said.

"Are many of them this easy?" I asked.

"Lots of them are, at this stage. Some that start out like this wake up later, and give you trouble then. Every horse is different," Blue said simply.

"I sure appreciate your helping me," I told him, as we led Danny back to the barn.

"No problem." Blue smiled. "I want to help you, Stormy. And I'd like to stay with you. But I need to go back to the farm and check on some more baby roses. Can I call you tonight?"

"Of course," I said, and was conscious of a feeling of disappointment that he was leaving. Another little roll in the hay sounded good to me.

"See you soon," Blue said, and got in his truck.

I put Danny away and walked up the hill to the house. The air was hot and dry, yesterday's cloud cover vanished as if it had never been. It was time, I thought, for fire season to be over. Time for rain.

At the thought, I was reminded of Christy George. Turning away from my front door, I got in my truck instead. Maybe I'd take a drive to Harkins Valley.

THIRTEEN

Christy George's place was a mess. Firefighters and police were everywhere, and the barn was cordoned off with yellow tape. Jeri Ward and Walt Harvey stood together, talking to two men. Christy was out in the driveway with a group of about half a dozen gathered around her. Among them were Clay and Bart Bishop.

The sight of Clay sent a little frisson of nerves down my spine. What, exactly, was I going to say to the man? Surely I owed him some kind of explanation if I wasn't going to date him anymore.

I approached Christy and her group.

"Hi Gail," Christy greeted me.

"How's it going?" I asked her.

"All right, all things considered. These kind folks are getting ready to haul the rest of my boarders off. Most of them left this morning already."

"Oh," I said. "Where are they going?"

"Here and there. This last lot are mostly going to Bart's place."

"Do you have room?" I asked Bart curiously.

"Oh yeah. We had some people leave, after the fire. I've got room. These horses will only be with us temporarily. They're going back here as soon as Christy rebuilds." He smiled at Christy as he said it.

She gave him a weak smile in return. "It's going to take awhile," she said. She gestured at Jeri and Walt's little group. "Those insurance people have to make up their minds what and if they're going to pay me."

"Surely they'll pay you," I said.

"It depends on whether they think I burned my own barn down," she said glumly.

"After two fires in a row?" I said in surprise.

"Who knows?" she shrugged.

"How are all the horses doing?" I asked. I could feel Clay's eyes on me as I spoke, but I kept my attention on Christy, not looking at him.

"Some are coughing. The one with burns seems to be doing okay."

"How about Clifford?" I asked her.

"He's fine. Thank God." Christy smiled at me. "Thanks again, Gail."

"No problem," I said. In the pause that followed, I finally brought myself to meet Clay's eyes.

He smiled at me with warmth, and I felt an immediate rush of guilt. Dammit, I told myself, I've done nothing wrong. I don't owe Clay anything.

Be that as it might, I still felt guilty. I needed to have a talk with Clay. But not now. Now I wanted to talk to Jeri.

Excusing myself, I moved in Jeri's direction, intercepting her as she walked toward her car with Walt.

"Hi, Gail." Jeri's smile was friendly.

Walt Harvey said nothing.

"Was this arson?" I asked her.

"We think so."

"Same method?"

"We think so," she said again.

"Did you ever check into that guy I pointed out to you?"

She thought a minute. "Larry Rogers," she said crisply. "Middle-aged, curly hair, glasses, overweight."

"That's him."

"I talked to him. He lives in the Lushmeadows subdivision. He readily admitted having watched the Bishop Ranch barn burn as well. At least half the people I spoke to had the same story. Why are you so interested in him?"

"His face, I guess. He looked almost delighted, watching the fires."

Walt Harvey shook his head at me. "That's not so unusual. Lots of people look enthralled, staring at a big fire. There's just something about it."

I nodded. "Know what you mean. But this guy's face was different somehow." I hesitated. "Do you think," I addressed Walt Harvey directly, "these two fires were set by the same person?"

He glanced at Jeri, who nodded imperceptibly.

Walt Harvey lifted one shoulder. "Yeah," he said. "Same method. An amateur almost for sure. Pretty unlikely it would be two different people unless this one is a copycat fire. And if it is, the copycat would have to know just how the first fire was started."

"Are you still looking at Marty Martin?" I asked Jeri.

"That's where we're going now," she said.

"Well, do me a favor, just for old times' sake," I said. "Check into this Larry Rogers. My intuition just shouts at me about him."

"All right." Jeri smiled at me. "You've been right before." And she and Walt Harvey climbed into the car.

I was headed for my own truck when I felt a hand on my shoulder. It was Clay.

"Aren't you even going to say hi?" he asked.

"Hi, Clay." I smiled, but I knew it was forced.

"Where are you off to?"

"Home. I've got a colt I'm breaking," I ad-libbed, not knowing why I felt I had to explain myself.

"Oh. Would you like to go out to dinner tonight?"

"I'm sorry. I've got plans." I hoped I had plans, anyway.

"All right," Clay said easily. "Give me a call, then." He moved off to help Brother Bart load a horse into the stock trailer.

Well, I thought. If I keep on sounding as inane and off-putting as I just did there, I may not have to explain anything to Clay. He'll quit pursuing me of his own accord.

I watched Bart and Clay finish loading horses and get into their rig, then got into my own truck and started to turn around. My progress was halted by yet another vehicle pulling in. Hans Schmidt.

Hans pulled his truck up next to mine; we both rolled down our windows.

"Ah, the lovely Dr. McCarthy," he said.

I could feel myself gritting my teeth. Why in hell did most women seem to find this man so charming?

"Hi, Hans," I said. "What's up?"

"I have come to check on my patients."

"I think all the horses have been moved," I told him. "Some to the Bishop Ranch, some to other places."

"That is too bad. I had meant to suggest that my client give her horse a vacation at Quail Run."

"Is that right?"

"It would have been ideal for him. Horses are not meant to live in this sort of confinement, you know. It is inhumane to keep them in these little boxes."

I stared at him for a long minute. "Right," I said. "If you'd move your truck just a little—I was about to leave. Another call, you know."

"Of course." Hans gave me a courtly smile and pulled his truck forward.

I sighed in my relief. It was getting hard for me to be polite to this guy.

Pulling out of Christy's driveway, I let the truck drift toward home, resisting the impulse to drive out to the rose farm. Surely I could go a few hours without seeing Blue.

But when I stepped out into my own yard, the place seemed desolate. Not just Blue's absence—even the weather seemed to conspire against me. The sky was a diffuse, milky color; the sun looked brassy. It was still warm, but wind tossed the crown of the big eucalyptus, flinging the leaves about noisily. The shaggy pale pink trunks gleamed ghostly white in the odd light.

It was hard to concentrate on chores, though there were plenty that needed doing. I watered my potted plants in a desultory way and wished that Blue would call.

Already I felt empty without him; my little house looked forlorn and lonely, perched on the side of its hill. Such a shift, and in only a day. I thought of Jade Hudson, content on her solitary knoll, but it did no good. I wanted Blue's company.

Not just any company—Blue's company. Somehow, I wasn't quite sure how, I had managed to fall head-over-heels into love after one brief tumble in the hay. They don't call it making love for nothing, I thought wryly.

Finding that I was staring off into space, watering can in hand, I yielded to Roey's entreaties and picked up her tennis ball. Over and over again, I sent the ball flying across the open space next to the vegetable garden while Roey dashed after it.

Blue could park his trailer here, I thought.

My God, I was already moving him in, after just one night of passion. But the thought remained.

Calling to Roey, I walked back to the house, my mind busily chattering at me. Are you crazy, Gail? You can't just make an impulse buy of a man, as if he were a horse, or a dog.

Why not, I rebutted. I've known him awhile. He's not going to turn out to be an ax murderer or anything.

Or an arsonist. The thought arose. I stopped to consider it. I did not fear that Blue Winter was anything other than the kind and decent man he had consistently appeared to be. But the person who had burned two barns down and killed three horses; did he appear kind and decent to his nearest and dearest, too?

I knew nothing about the crime of arson, nothing about arsonists. Somehow the thought was unsettling.

Turning back to my first premise, I reassured myself that offering to rent Blue some space to park his trailer was not tantamount to a lifelong commitment. I would merely be, in a certain sense, his landlord.

Yeah, right. What the hell, I told myself. What the hell.

FOURTEEN

Monday morning I was late. Blue had come by to take me to dinner the night before and one thing led to another. It was a lot harder to drag myself out of a warm, cozy bed and away from a lover's kisses than it was to leave my solitary dwelling. Not to mention, I then had to swing by my own home to change clothes and feed the animals.

I drove into the office parking lot at eight o'clock, feeling disorganized and disheveled. John Romero was just parking his truck in my accustomed spot.

For some reason, this was the last straw. Getting out of my pickup, I called to his departing back, "John. We need to talk."

He stopped and turned, looking less than pleased.

"I'm having a problem with your behavior," I said. "You seem to resent me. I'd like to talk about it, see if we can come to a better working arrangement."

John stared at me. "What's the problem?" he said at last.

My turn to stare. This guy was an absolute mystery to me. Why on earth was he being such an ass?

"Why are you acting like such an ass?" I said.

I saw a flash of anger deep in his eyes, as hard and bright as his habitual expression was clouded and sulky.

"Why do you think your shit doesn't stink?" he said.

"What?"

"You're so goddamn arrogant," he said flatly. "You think every judgment you make is automatically right."

"Is that how you see me?" I was very honestly surprised. "I sure don't mean to come off like that." I thought about it. "Let me ask you something, John," I said. "Does my manner annoy you because I'm a woman? And you think a little bit before you answer that. I know I can be pretty blunt and I don't beat around the bush much, but a lot of guys are like that, including our mutual boss. Jim's never been one for the polite routine, and you don't seem to mind him."

John said nothing.

I went on. "Once in a while I meet a guy who thinks that women are supposed to be more conciliating than men, just because they're women. In other words, if Jim's looking at a lame horse with you and he snaps out, 'Left fore,' and turns away, it's fine, but if I do the same thing it's arrogant. Because I'm a woman and women aren't supposed to talk that way. Especially to men."

John kept on staring at me and saying nothing.

"Let's cut to the chase here." I met his eyes. "I don't mean to be arrogant. I can be wrong, and it's fine to point it out to me. But I expect you to cut me the same slack you would cut Jim or any other man in a position of authority over you. It is not my obligation to phrase things differently because I'm female. And you may not like working for and with a woman, but you need to get one thing straight. As long as you're working here, you're working for me as well as Jim. I'm the junior partner and I am your boss."

I stopped to let him speak, but he wasn't buying. Just kept that silent gaze unwaveringly on my face.

"Is there anything you would like to say to me?" I asked him.

"No," he said. "May I go now? Boss?"

I stared, looking for a gleam of humor, but I saw nothing I could recognize. His expression was flatter than ever.

"Sure," I said, and watched him turn away.

108

What was going on here? My attempt to get things straight didn't seem to have done any good at all. I didn't understand this guy, hadn't a clue about how to begin to understand him. As far as I was concerned, I might need to get a degree in psychology just to get an inkling.

Bingo. The answer came to me in a rush. This evening I told myself, wait till this evening.

At five o'clock I presented myself at Dr. Alan Todd's place of business, keeping my monthly appointment. When my depression had lifted, just before the trip to Europe, I'd considered terminating my relationship with this doctor. I hadn't done it, though. Some inner sense had told me I still needed his input.

I'd listened. More and more I was learning to listen to this small, still voice, though voice was really a misnomer. It was more of an intuition, a knowing without words, simply a sense of what was best. Nothing like the constant chatter of my busy, busy mind, this quiet guide merely led me where I needed to go.

Had it led me into bed with Blue Winter? And was it now leading me toward offering him a berth? I contemplated these questions as I sat in Dr. Todd's waiting room.

When my shrink opened his office door, I was deep in thought and almost jumped at the sight of him.

"Dr. McCarthy, welcome." As was his custom, Dr. Todd smiled and held out his hand.

I shook it. "Dr. Todd. Good to see you."

Dr. Alan Todd looked much as usual. Dark blue slacks, light blue shirt, brown V-necked sweater with a small but obvious hole in it. Chartreuse tie, tassels on his loafers. An East Coast preppie with an iconoclastic twist. Like his car, an old Dodge Dart, Dr. Todd was unpredictable.

I walked into his office and chose my usual chair. Dr. Todd sat facing me in his desk chair, with his back to the desk and a manila folder in his lap. From time to time he made a note on a paper in the folder. Business as usual.

Finishing up my romantic saga, I said, "So I seem to have chosen to get involved with Blue, though I'm hardly sure how

I did it. I'm trying to decide whether to invite him to move his trailer out to my place. Also, what I'm going to say to Clay."

Dr. Todd's eyes twinkled. "You sound happy," he said.

"I do?" I thought about it. "I am happy."

"Sounds like you're moving in the right direction to me."

"It's not that I don't have problems," I went on. "I just recognize that they're not the end of the world. Like this guy at work." And I told him the whole story of John Romero and his attitude.

"Where does that come from and how do I deal with it?" I asked.

"Hmmm." Dr. Todd folded his hands with his fingertips together. "I would say that you need to know a little bit about this man's family background to know why he acts like this."

"Is that what it always comes down to? The old family-of-origin thing?"

"More or less." Dr. Todd smiled. "It is fairly primary. What happens to us when we are babies and young children shapes our view of life thereafter. It's the basis we come from. It's our ground."

"So, do men like John, who appear to dislike women, all have some sort of 'bad' mother?"

"You could say that, as a guess. I wouldn't use the word 'bad,' but I would say such men probably didn't feel comfortably close and connected to their mothers."

"How does a man get to feeling close and connected to his mother?"

"In my opinion," Dr. Todd smiled again, "it's very simple and primitive. Of course, not everyone will agree with this. But my view is that that connection is established in the very beginning of life when the mother fulfills the baby's deep expectations, which are bred into him, so to speak."

"How does that work?"

"We're just fancy monkeys." Dr. Todd wrinkled his nose at me. "What I mean is that we are, in certain senses, a kind of animal. Our babies, like little monkeys, expect to be carried everywhere the mother goes, to sleep next to the mother at night, to nurse whenever the baby is hungry. When these simple expectations are met, babies feel close and connected to their mothers.

"It gets more complicated as a child gets older; sons need to know their mothers respect them—at the same time their mothers are there to protect them. All children need to feel that they are seen and accepted for who they are; mothers who are able to let go of their own needs and expectations and who are willing to help their children shape their own destinies do these children a big favor. In other words, mothers who aren't too controlling are most helpful to children, particularly sons."

"And if a mother is very controlling?"

"There is almost always resentment, which gets acted out in various ways."

At his words, a thought occurred to me. "Is arson one of those ways?"

"Arson? Do you feel this man at work is practicing arson?" Dr. Todd sounded shocked, as well he might.

"No, no. It's just that there is an arsonist in my neighborhood, more or less, someone who's burning down horse barns. I've gotten somewhat involved. Professionally," I added hastily. "I was just wondering the other day if there is a typical psychological profile for an arsonist."

Dr. Todd nodded. "I don't know a great deal about this—it's not my area of specialty—but yes, there are a few well-accepted premises. Arsonists are almost always male, and often, there is some kind of sexual dysfunction. The arsonist gets his sexual kick out of setting fires because he feels in some way frustrated with women."

"Would that imply a 'bad' mother?" I asked flippantly.

"An overly controlling and/or needy mother is a common factor with men who have problems with women," Dr. Todd agreed. "Of course, I believe most arson is for profit, not for psychological reasons."

"I suppose that's right." I thought of Larry Rogers and his rapt expression. "Do arsonists, those arsonists with psychological motivations, anyway, take delight in the sight of their fires?"

"I believe so. They are commonly part of the watching crowd, and may even take a part in putting the fire out and rescuing people. Going back to your original premise," Dr. Todd went on, "many men who are hostile to women and/or have problems with sexual dysfunction do have difficult relationships with their mothers. Unfortunately, in our society, such difficulties are fairly common."

"So, what should I do, if I'm trying to work with a man like that? Just looking at me seems to make him mad. It must have something to do with the fact that I'm his boss. By all accounts he doesn't act that way with female clients."

"A woman in a position of authority over him would certainly trigger any issues he has with his mother," Dr. Todd said quietly. "He feels comfortably in charge, perhaps, when dealing with women as clients."

"Any suggestions? I tried to straighten things out by being direct, and it didn't work at all."

"My guess would be that anything forceful in your manner would be difficult for him."

I looked at Dr. Todd and sighed. "That's just the problem. I have a fairly direct way of speaking, especially in my role at work. I've cultivated it; clients feel more comfortable with a veterinarian who sounds as if he or she is in charge. Especially if that vet is a young woman." I smiled. "Well, middle-aged, now.

"On top of that, my boss is so blunt as to be downright rude at times, and I may have developed a similar style after working with him for seven years. And I think you're right. I think it gets on this guy John's nerves. I'm just not sure I want to try to modify myself for him."

Dr. Todd nodded.

"It really irks me," I went on, "to deal with men who have to be baby-sat like that. They find a competent, forthright woman completely threatening."

"It must be frustrating."

"It is. And it's one thing to mollycoddle a client who's like that—it's part of my job to get along with clients. But it's entirely another thing when the guy concerned is working for me."

"Can you terminate him?"

"Maybe." I sighed again. "It would be so much easier and better for all of us if John and I could just get along."

"My guess would be you might need to mollycoddle him a little, as you put it. Flatter him." Dr. Todd smiled at me.

I didn't smile back. "It just pisses me off. That's part of the problem. I have just as much anger at the notion that I need to be extra careful and polite to John simply because I'm female as he seems to have at the idea that he has to work for me. It's one of my own issues, I guess. I try to treat people fairly, and I do my best to be a good person, but I do not feel it is part of my role in life to kiss men's asses, simply because I'm a woman."

Dr. Todd nodded.

"Does this make me hostile?" I asked him.

"Not in my opinion. Not as an overall position. You can be hostile, certainly, but I do not see you as a hostile person. You are a fairly blunt person, and that can be difficult for some personality types to deal with."

"I know. I guess I'm just going to have to wait awhile, see what seems right to do. What about my new romance and how to tell Clay?" I added.

"Just follow your instincts," Dr. Todd said.

"That doesn't sound like typical shrink advice to me."

"I'm not a typical shrink." His eyes twinkled as he stood up.

"That's right, you're not." I stood up, also. "Thank you," I said.

"You're very welcome."

I turned to go but his voice stopped me. "These arson fires, do they have a pattern?"

"Well, there've only been two. They were both in the hay barns of stables in Harkins Valley. And according to the fire investigator, the arsonist used the same method both times."

"Any other similarities?"

I thought about it. "They were both on a Friday evening."

"Do you live in Harkins Valley?" he asked.

"No. Not far away, but I don't actually live in the valley. Why?"

"I think," he said slowly, "if I had horses and I lived in Harkins Valley, I'd be watchful this Friday night. Very watchful."

"I see what you mean," I said.

113

FIFTEEN

Friday turned out to be my day for emergencies. The first call that morning was Jade Hudson.

"She's got a horse she needs you to put down," Nancy told me.

"Tell her I'll be right there." Turning, I went back out and climbed into the truck I had just vacated. From what little I knew of Jade Hudson, I was willing to bet she would not make such a phone call unless it were necessary.

Arriving at her place half an hour later, I found her waiting in the yard.

"One of my old boys went down yesterday morning and won't get up," she said. "He doesn't seem to be suffering, but I think twenty-four hours is long enough."

"Do you want to try and find out what's going on with him?" I asked her.

"I don't think so. This horse is thirty-two years old and he's been in a decline for the last month or so. He hasn't seemed too interested in his feed; he's been moving slower and slower and not staying with the others. I think it's time."

"All right," I said. "Let me get the shot ready."

Once the syringe was full, I followed Jade into the pasture.

She marched steadily through the damp brownish tan stubble, headed eastward; as we topped a rise, I saw the gray horse lying on his belly in the hollow ahead of us.

Jade walked up to him and stroked his neck. The horse looked at her calmly.

"Well, Rodney," she said, "I think it's time, don't you?"

She crouched next to him and put a halter on his head. Rubbing his ears, she looked him in the eyes for a long moment.

"All right," she said to me.

I crouched beside her. Patting the gray's neck, I injected the kill shot into his jugular vein. Jade Hudson continued to stroke him while I did it.

"I love you," she said softly to the horse. Tears were running quietly down her face, but she seemed calm.

"Are you all right?" I asked her.

"I'm fine," she said. "I always cry, because it is sad, but I'm fine with it. I know it's time."

After a minute, Rodney lifted his head slightly. There was a brief alarm in his eyes; Jade and I both readied ourselves to get out of the way if he started thrashing. Mercifully, he didn't.

Slowly his head lowered and his eyes seemed to dim. Laying his muzzle down on the ground, he folded over onto his side. His ribs moved once with the last breath. Jade Hudson continued to stroke his neck.

After another minute, I used my stethoscope to listen for a heartbeat.

"All quiet," I told her. "He's gone."

She nodded, the tears still flowing. "Thank you," she said.

"Sure you're okay?"

"I'm sure." Straightening up, she stood beside me. "I've been through this before. I'm accepting of it. Death is part of life."

"True enough," I said.

For a long moment I gazed at her quiet, tear-streaked face. I saw the serenity, the peace. Even as I looked at her, I knew that her tranquillity was born, at least in part, from the solitary, monastic simplicity of her life. I knew this, because in some ways my life resembled hers. And now I was giving it up.

Blue's face came into my mind, the memory of his touch, his kisses. Even the thought of him sent a surge of basic, primitive desire through me. I already knew, somewhere deep inside, that I was giving up the solitary life for Blue. There was no doubt in my gut.

Jade and I walked back to my pickup together. "Thank you," she said again, as I climbed in.

"You're welcome."

I could see her in my rearview mirror as I drove out, her head bent slightly, walking back to her house. And then my cell phone rang.

"Gail, Tony Sanchez has a colic," Nancy said.

"I'll be right there."

Tony lived in Harkins Valley, just down the road from Christy George. As I drove the narrow, winding curves of Harkins Valley Road, I passed one horse operation after another. Harkins Valley was ideal horse country and many, if not most, of the folks who moved out here were horse people. The options were endless: On the right a high-class jumper stable with all new facilities, on the left a little old family farm that belonged to Judith Rainier, the barbed-wire-fenced pastures full of rodeo horses. Next came a turn-of-the-century dairy converted to a setup for a woman who raised Shetland ponies, and then the wide, white-board-fenced fields of a local dot-com millionaire. In the distance I could see the plots of horsey Lushmeadows subdivision. Tony Sanchez's place was on the right.

Tony had money. He owned pricey cutting horses—about a dozen of them—and was one of our best clients. His peach-colored Spanish-style house was new, as was the modern metal barn and corral setup behind it. One large pasture was fenced in non-climb wire with an iron-pipe top rail. Everything perfectly tidy. I drove up to the barn. Tony was waiting for me in front of a box stall.

In his early fifties, or so I guessed, of medium height and a Mexican heritage, Tony had the high cheekbones, broad planed face and dark olive complexion of his Indian forefathers. He also had a wide, white smile and tons of ambition. Tony was one of the most successful electrical contractors in Santa Cruz County.

I climbed out of my truck and walked to greet him. "Hi Tony," I said. "How are you?"

Tony held out his hand and I shook it. "I am fine. And you, Gail?"

"Doing well," I said. "How is your mother?"

"She is doing well, also. Thank you for asking."

Tony spoke English perfectly, with only the slightest trace of a Mexican accent. Meticuously polite himself, he appreciated a certain formal politeness in others, something I had learned over the years. No matter how dire the situation, Tony would want to conduct a decorous ritual greeting.

"Well, please give her my regards," I said to him now. "I always enjoy Doña Esther." This last was quite true. Tony's mother lived with him, and I had met her several times. A sprightly, intense woman, some eighty-five years young, she took a lively interest in the horses, and could often be seen out at the barn, gesturing in an imperious way with one small, claw-like hand as she pointed out chores that needed doing.

"I will tell her you said so." Tony smiled. "I am sure she will be very pleased."

Feeling that the forms had been taken care of, I gestured at the stall door Tony was standing in front of. "You have a problem?"

"Yes, this horse has been having little stomach aches for a week. But today, he is worse."

"Uh-oh." Little colics off and on for a week usually meant one of two things: sand or stones. Neither was desirable, though stones were a good deal more lethal than sand.

"Let's have a look at him," I said.

The strawberry roan gelding was cross-tied in his stall. Head hanging down, he pawed the shavings beneath him repetitively. In his eyes was a look of dull misery.

After checking his vital signs, I bent over and had a long listen to his gut. Finally I stood up and faced Tony.

"Sand or a stone?" he asked with a wry smile. Tony was a horseman; he probably knew almost as much about colics as I did.

"I'm not sure," I said. "You can usually hear sand in the gut, and I can't. And, judging by his vital signs, which are pretty good, it's probably not a stone."

"I hope it is not that." Tony sighed.

We both knew that stones, an odd anomaly that seems to occur only on the West Coast—no one really knows why—could only be cured by expensive, and risky, surgery. "Stones," when removed, looked exactly like stones—round, smooth river rocks—and could be six inches or more in diameter. They were thought to be coagulations of some sort of mineral build-up in a horse's intestines. A given animal could carry one or more stones around for a long time, years even, and then a stone would shift into a spot where it blocked all passage through the intestine. An instant, and severe, colic resulted. Such colics often ended in torsions, or twists, where the intestine behaves like a hose with a kink in it. Only surgery—or a miracle—can save a horse with a twisted gut.

However, stones often gave warning as they moved around inside a horse, and the type of chronic, low-grade, persistent colic Tony had described to me was sometimes a sign of stones.

"I'm not sure," I said again. "I think what we ought to do is give him some painkiller, and pump some mineral oil into him, and then I want to run some blood work on him. Once in a while this sort of chronic colic turns out to be caused by an internal infection."

"I have never heard of that," Tony said. "What do you do?"

"Antibiotics can usually clear it up."

"That is good."

"You'd better put him on a regime of psyllium, too," I said. "Just in case he does have some sand in there. The extra fiber can help."

"I can do that," Tony said. "I have some psyllium in the feed room."

I finished the procedures of injecting painkiller into the horse's jugular vein and pumping mineral oil through a tube I inserted in his nostril and down his esophagus. As Tony was walking me out to my truck, I spotted Doña Esther, waving to me from one of the windows in the house. I waved back.

"Be sure to tell your mother I said hi," I told Tony.

"I will," he agreed. "Would you care to come in? She always enjoys company."

"I would love to, but I have a busy day ahead of me."

"I understand." Tony flashed his very white smile at me. "Any time you would care to visit, my mother and I would be delighted. I think she is sometimes lonely."

"Living with you?" I smiled.

Tony shrugged. "I am glad I can give her such a life. We were very poor when I was a child. Now she can have anything she wants. But I think she misses her village."

"It's wonderful that you can do all this for her." I waved a hand at the surroundings.

He shrugged again, spreading his own hands out eloquently. "Surely it is what every son would want to do for his mother?"

I wondered. It seemed to me that quite a few adult sons wanted principally to avoid their mothers. And I had seen Doña Esther ordering Tony about in her charming but quite dictatorial way. I thought there might be many men who wouldn't care for that. Not to mention the fact that Tony was never known to date, a subject of some speculation in the local horse community. Rumor had it that his mother forbade it.

Before I could say anything else, my cell phone rang.

"Gail, Laurie Brown has a horse that she thinks may have eaten twenty-five to forty pounds of grain. He's not showing any problem yet, but . . ."

"I'll be right there," I said.

Laurie Brown lived in Harkins Valley, barely a mile from where I stood. Like Tony, she was one of our best clients. Unlike Tony, she did not possess a lot of sangfroid when it came to her horses.

Laurie's five Peruvian Pasos resembled the spoiled children of an indulgent mother. All possible luxuries and safeguards were provided for them; as a result, they seemed to acquire every malady and have every accident known to man or horse. As Laurie had once put it, "I could lock them in padded stalls and they'd find a way to hang themselves."

I pulled out of Tony's driveway at a good brisk clip, picturing Laurie Brown's likely hysteria, and waved at Lucy Kaplan, who was schooling a dressage horse in her riding ring. Lucy was a trainer who rented the place across the road from Tony. An old barn, it was known as Harkins Valley Stables, and had been the home of many different trainers over the years. These days Lucy's upscale clients, many of them from Lushmeadows, parked their BMWs, Mercedes, and Porsches in the little gravel lot next to the barn.

Cruising down Harkins Valley Road as fast as seemed safe, I wondered how one of Laurie Brown's pampered babies had gotten into the grain. Given her zealous care, it seemed an improbable accident.

In another minute, I passed the burned-out shell of Christy George's barn, no one about. Just before I reached Lushmeadows, I turned right on a short cul-de-sac called Redtail Ridge. Laurie Brown lived at the end of the road.

Laurie's place sat in the lap of the hills to the east of Harkins Valley proper. Her gently rolling five acres faced south and west; her small house, surrounded on all four sides by a porch, was at the back of the property, just below the ridge line. The barn and corrals were situated on the level land beneath it.

Laurie was waiting at her barn. Predictably, she could be seen pacing up and down in front of a stall as I drove in, peering at the horse inside.

Before I could even get out of the truck, she began talking. "He seems fine, Gail, but I'm not sure how much grain he ate and my book said to have the vet out, anyway."

"Your book's right," I told her. "The time to treat founder is before it happens, not after. After is often too late."

"What do you mean?" Laurie asked nervously.

"The onset of founder can take twelve hours or so," I explained. "By the time a horse shows pain, the laminae of his feet can already be so inflamed that irreversible bone damage will follow, no matter what we do."

"Oh no." Laurie seemed ready to burst out sobbing. "This is my favorite horse."

"When did he eat the grain?" I asked.

"Sometime between when I fed last night and when I came down to feed this morning. I can't believe he got into it. The sack had been sitting outside his stall for weeks. Right here." She pointed to a spot that certainly looked a safe distance away from the denizen of the stall, an alert-appearing chocolate brown gelding.

"I was feeding him a handful of grain with every feeding," she said. "Just to perk him up a little. And somehow, last night, he managed to reach that sack and drag it into the stall with him. When I got down here this morning I found the empty sack, inside the stall. I'm not sure exactly how much he ate. It was a fifty-pound sack and I think it was at least half-full."

"All right," I said calmly. "Here's what we're going to do. I'll check him over carefully; get a baseline evaluation on him. Then we'll tube him full of mineral oil, to move the grain through him, and I want to give him an anti-inflammatory and a relaxant. I'll inject them in the muscle. You'll need to repeat those doses this evening. With luck, he'll be just fine."

"I hope so."

"What's his name?" I asked her, as she got him out of his stall.

"Coco," she said, and launched off into a spiel about the horse's history and how wonderful he was.

I encouraged her to talk. Focusing on her horse's good points seemed to calm her a little, and this was, after all, part of my job. Being a good veterinarian involves having good people skills. One needs not only to doctor the animal, but also to have the owner feel happy about it.

This was something I had grown better at over the years. I'd learned to read clients as individuals; rather than producing the same pacific manner for all, I responded to each as the situation seemed to demand.

Tony, for instance, needed no bromides. Laurie, on the other hand, appreciated being distracted from her worry. Since I knew both these clients, it was easy to respond to them; more difficult was assessing a new person. Still, it needed to be done, and done well, if we were to continue to succeed as a practice.

As I checked Coco out—he appeared to be fine—and administered prophylactic measures, I reflected that people skills were Hans Schmidt's stock in trade. He attempted, often successfully, to charm clients; he flirted ostentatiously with any who were female, irrespective of age and manner. Jim and I were both a good deal less forthcoming—perhaps this was part of the reason we were losing people to Hans.

And what about John? I had no idea how he related to clients.

Making a snap decision, I asked Laurie, "Have you used our new vet?"

"Yes. A couple of times. John, right?"

"Right. Between you and me, what do you think?"

Laurie furrowed her brow. She might be a bit obsessive about her horses, but in real life, so to speak, Laurie Brown was an extremely successful, and very sharp, businesswoman. Her opinion would be useful. I waited quietly while she thought.

"He's all right," she said. "He took care of the two problems I had him out for—they were minor—very competently. He had a pretty good way with the horses. It was just . . ." She paused.

"What?" I asked.

"He was so quiet," she said. "Very polite, but I couldn't read him at all. Couldn't tell if he liked me or despised me, if you know what I mean. I found it a bit disconcerting."

"Yes," I said. "Thank you. And I think Coco will be all right. There's no sign of a problem, and we've done all the right things. Be sure and call me if he shows any reluctance to move around or any sign of pain. Right away," I added.

"I'll do that," she said.

I climbed back in my truck, waving good-bye. I hadn't made it out her front gate before my cell phone rang again.

"Gail, Amber St. Claire's got a bad puncture wound on her young stallion. She wants you up there right away."

"Great," I said. "All right."

Amber St. Claire was one of my least favorite clients. She was rich and spoiled and raised Quarter Horses. That about covered it for me, as far as descriptions were concerned. Amber could be counted on to be difficult.

Today was no exception. My arrival at her place was greeted by a curt, "Where've you been?"

"It took me an hour to get here from Harkins Valley," I said evenly. "It's just that far. Morning, Amber."

She lifted her chin in a brief acknowledgment of my greeting and turned away. I followed her out to the barn.

Amber's young stallion stood cross-tied in the barn aisle. Dark chestnut, he had the lean, breedy look of a Quarter Horse with running bloodlines, which means, in essence, mostly Thoroughbred. Something about the sharp, steely look in his eyes made me wrinkle my nose. His knee was as big as a football.

"When did it happen?" I asked.

"Yesterday. It's a puncture. Pretty deep," Amber said. No mention of why she hadn't called us out yesterday, I noticed.

"You know the drill," I told her. "I'm going to need to flush it out, maybe x-ray it to look for foreign bodies and bone chips, and then we'll start him on a regime of antibiotics and flushing." I gave the horse a dubious look. "How's he going to be about all this?"

"Tee?" she laughed. "He's a big baby. I'll get Jill to help you." Cupping her hands, she whistled sharply.

A minute or two later, a plump girl came trudging in from somewhere.

"Jill, hold this horse for Gail." Amber waved a preemptory hand.

Jill was almost certainly stable help; still, as usual, Amber's manner was more that of master to slave than employer to employee. I waited for Jill to untie the horse; it had never crossed my mind that Amber would hold him herself. Many years of experience had taught me that Amber didn't get her hands dirty. She liked queening it around in the horse world; she did not like work.

123

Jill put the chestnut stallion on a lead line while Amber strolled off down the barn aisle.

"How's he going to be about this?" I asked the woman quietly, as Amber moved out of earshot. I noticed that Jill was handling Tee with considerable caution.

She shook her head. "Don't take your eyes off of him," she warned. "He acts quiet and sweet, and then, bang, he goes for you. He's the most dangerous stud I've ever been around. He almost killed me last week. Grabbed for my neck when I wasn't looking. I was wearing a jacket and I moved quick; that's the only reason I'm here. He ripped my jacket right in two."

"Geez," I said. "Amber said he was a pup."

"That's what she told me, too," Jill snorted. " 'Tee's just a big baby.' T. Rex is what I call him."

"Right," I said. Keeping one careful eye on the stallion's face, I injected a solid dose of tranquilizer into his jugular vein. In a minute he was swaying on his feet.

"That ought to do it," I told Jill, who visibly relaxed.

In a minute Amber was back. "What's with Tee?" she snapped. "You didn't tranquilize him, did you? He doesn't need that."

"I'm afraid I won't work on a stallion without tranquilizing him, Amber," I said blandly. "Too many bad experiences, you know."

"Are you afraid of him?"

"That's right," I agreed. "I am afraid to get hurt."

Amber shrugged derisively, the wind taken out of her sails. "Get on with it, then."

I did. Heavily sedated, T. Rex posed no problem. I gave Jill antibiotics and instructions and took my leave, feeling sorry for her. Halfway back to the office, the phone rang again.

"Gail, I just got a call about a broken leg." Nancy sounded apologetic.

"Damn. Where is it?"

"Felton." Nancy gave me directions and I headed off in that direction, after canceling my scheduled appointments. It was past noon; I already knew it was one of those days.

The broken leg turned out to be a sole abscess, a vastly more fixable problem, thank God; it was followed by two more colics, a bowed tendon, and then a bad wire cut. At nine o'clock I was in the middle of a complicated stitching job when the phone call came in from the answering service.

The usually prosaic operator sounded breathless. "Harkins Valley Stable has a barn fire. They need you right away."

SIXTEEN

I can't come," I said. "I've got to finish this job. Call John Romero; tell him I need him to cover. I'll be there as soon as I can."

I hung up the phone with a rush of adrenaline surging through my veins. Another barn fire in Harkins Valley on a Friday night. This made three in a row. Some very sick person was setting horse barns on fire. To a pattern.

Taking a deep breath, I consciously relaxed all my muscles and went back to the job in front of me. This two-year-old filly had gotten her hind leg caught in a barbed-wire fence, and had struggled, unsuccessfully, to free her herself. Her leg was deeply lacerated, almost to the bone in places. Worst of all, her hock was severely cut. There was no way of knowing how badly the joint was injured without X rays, which the owner refused to have, saying they cost too much. He just wanted the mare stitched back together.

Just patching her up was going to be an expensive job in itself, but I didn't tell him that. Judging by the sagging shed and falling-down pen where he kept the horse, he was probably short of money. I resolved to do the stitching, which badly needed doing, and worry about the bill later.

It took a good long time. Almost half an hour after the phone call, I finished her up. Brushing aside the client's protests about the cost, I told him we'd send him a bill and to pay what he could each month. He was still talking as I got in my truck and left.

Twenty minutes later I was driving down Harkins Valley Road, with the light from Lucy Kaplan's barn fire visible through my windshield—an orangy glow on the dark horizon. In another minute, I pulled in her driveway and parked.

The scene was pure pandemonium. Once again, the leaping flames, the running horses, the struggling firefighters, and the frantic or enthralled crowd of owners, neighbors, and spectators. I spotted Tony Sanchez, clinging to a neighing horse; in another second I saw Bart Bishop dash out of the burning barn, two loose horses charging with him.

I scanned the crowd. Sure enough, there he was. Pudgy Larry, staring at the flames, rapt. There was something wrong with this guy; I knew it. Where the hell were Jeri and Walt?

Before I could begin to look, Clay Bishop grabbed my arm. "Gail, there's a horse with real bad burns, down in the ring."

"Coming," I said, and went.

Hans Schmidt and John Romero were already there. Both were staring at the horse. I knew by the expression on their faces what I would see. Slowly, I walked to join them.

The horse's whole body was a mass of burned flesh; I couldn't believe he was standing and appeared structurally intact. I looked at Hans and John in turn.

"What the heck do you do?" I asked softly.

Both shook their heads somberly.

Most of the horse's body appeared to be charred and flaking; he smelled of burned hair and meat. His face was undamaged, but I couldn't read the expression in his eyes. They seemed blank. He stood perfectly, rigidly still, as if frozen, his head down.

"I guess we could try hauling him to the equine hospital," I said slowly. "Whose horse is he?"

"Lucy's," Clay said. "That's what one of the boarders told me."

"Where is she?" I asked.

"She's not here," Clay said. "I guess she was gone when the fire started. She doesn't live here. Someone called her. She was in town, at a movie. She ought to be here any minute."

As if on cue, a white pickup pulled into the crowded driveway. Lucy Kaplan got out and ran toward the barn. For a moment she stood there, staring, and then turned and said something to the woman next to her. A minute later, I heard Lucy's scream from where I stood.

"Frank!"

I looked at the group around me. "Who's Frank?"

No one answered. Clay departed in Lucy's direction. Hans moved off after him. John and I stared at the horse's disfigured flesh.

"Better put him down," John said at last.

I nodded slowly. "I'll ask Lucy."

I started in the direction of the driveway and met Lucy coming toward me, guided by Clay. Lucy was in tears, sobbing so hard she was stumbling. Clay was trying to support her and pat her back at the same time.

"Oh, Frank, I'm so sorry," Lucy moaned.

"Who's Frank?" I asked Clay.

Clay looked at me. Even in the dark I could read the shock in his eyes. "A caretaker. An old man. He lives in the cottage behind the barn."

"Did the cottage burn?"

"No, it's fine. But no one's seen Frank. Lucy's sure he wouldn't have gone out. She thinks he must be in the barn."

"Oh no."

"She thinks he must have been trying to get the horses out and got trapped before anyone else got here. Tony Sanchez saw the fire and called 911," Clay said. "Then he called me and Bart and some other neighbors. No one's seen the old man. He's not in the cottage."

"Oh no," I said again.

"I'm sorry, Frank," Lucy said through her tears.

I put a hand on her arm, hating what I had to say next.

"There's a horse in the ring that's very badly burned. I understand he's yours. Do you want me to put him down? Or do you
want to consider having him hauled somewhere?"

"Oh my God." Lucy sounded as completely overwhelmed as
I ever imagined this very tough, thirtyish woman could sound.
"I better have a look, I guess," she said.

"I don't know," I said. "He looks pretty bad."

She gazed at me helplessly. "Can you save him?"

"It's possible," I said slowly, "that he could be saved. It would
be expensive and it would take a lot of time and he'd always be
disfigured."

"It's Clancy," Lucy said, as if talking to herself. "He'll never
be worth anything." Once again she looked at me. "Don't let
him suffer," she said finally.

"You want me to put him down?"

Lucy nodded, tears still running down her cheeks.

"All right."

Going out to my truck, I got the shot and then headed back.
John still stood there, holding the burned horse by the lead rope.

"She said to put him down," I said. "I think it's the right
choice."

He nodded wordlessly and got out of my way, taking a firmer
grip on the lead rope.

I stepped forward and found a spot on the underside of the
animal's neck that wasn't burned. Carefully, I inserted the needle
in the jugular vein and injected the shot. A minute later the horse
lurched forward, staggering and falling at once. Expertly, John
used the lead rope to steady the animal, easing the horse's fall
and encouraging him to go down at the same time. In another
minute, the horse was on the ground. His legs thrashed convul-
sively once and then he settled into stillness.

"Poor guy," I said slowly. This was the worst part of being a
vet. Facing these poor suffering animals that I couldn't save.

John said nothing, but his eyes never left the horse's burned
body.

We stood, in silence, until the howl of the inferno behind us
grabbed my attention. The roar and snarl of the fire carried over

the hubbub of human voices; incandescent, surging tongues reached high into the night sky. Smoke billowed outward. The barn was engulfed. Seething and snapping, the flames held me riveted. Like some huge, powerful beast, the fire coiled and leaped and bellowed. I could feel my mouth dropping open in awe.

"It's really something, isn't it?" John's quiet voice.

"Yeah," I said. "It's something, all right, and it's horrible, too. I've got to find somebody. Come get me if you need me."

I headed back toward the barn, looking for Jeri. It didn't take me long. She and Walt Harvey were right out front.

"That Larry guy," I said without preamble. "He's here."

"I know," she said. "So's Marty Martin. So is half the Lush-meadows subdivision, or I miss my guess."

I looked at Walt Harvey. "Fire number three," I said.

"Oh yeah." Walt looked excited. "We've got a real pyro here. A serial arsonist. You don't see too many of these."

"Do pyros," I asked, saying the word a little gingerly, "like to watch their fires burn?"

"Some do," he said. "What we call vanity arsonists. The ones who get their jollies out of fires, so to speak."

"Is this what's going on here?" I asked.

"Don't know yet," he said.

"But you do have a pattern," I said. "Friday night barn fires in Harkins Valley. All in the same neighborhood."

"That's right," he said slowly. "Friday night barn fires . . . that reminds me of something." He was quiet for a long moment and then he turned to Jeri. "I need to check my laptop. It's in the car. I'll be right back."

And he disappeared into the crowd of people in the drive.

I asked Jeri, "Have you checked Larry out yet?"

"We talked to him. He said his wife can give him an alibi for this evening. Same for the last two fires. He said he showed up when he heard the sirens—just like the rest of the crowd."

"Does an alibi from a wife count?"

Jeri shrugged. "It's better than nothing."

We both stared at the roaring flames in front of us. I could feel heat on my face. Small, struggling forms of firefighters looked trivial, silhouetted against the blaze.

"I hear there might be a man in there," I said slowly.

Jeri shook her head. "I sure hope not. Firefighters didn't see anyone. But then, they weren't really looking. By the time someone noticed the caretaker was missing, the fire had really taken off. No one can get in there now."

"If the caretaker is dead," I said, "is it murder?"

"That's right," Jeri said grimly. "Homicide for sure. Second-degree murder, probably, since I doubt our arsonist meant to kill anyone. Doesn't seem to be his pattern. But it's still murder."

"Speaking of patterns," I said, "do you know what Walt went to check on? I said 'pattern' and he disappeared."

"Walt's got an encyclopedic memory for fires. Whatever you said probably triggered something in his brain. He's really thorough, so he'll want to check it out before he says anything to me."

"So, who are you working on?" I asked her. "Marty Martin?"

"He's still suspect number one at this point. He's saying his parents can give him an alibi for tonight. He was at home until he heard the fire trucks, so he tells us. And I'm sure his folks will back him up. But like a wife, his parents aren't worth much as an alibi."

As she finished speaking, Walt Harvey emerged from the crowd on the drive. If he'd looked excited before, he now appeared delirious. Eyes shining, mouth parted, he grabbed Jeri by one elbow.

"Barn fires of '85!" he shouted.

Jeri grabbed his arm in return. "What?

"We had a series of barn fires in '85." Jim's face was six inches from Jeri's. "On Tuesday nights. Four of them. When we caught the guy, it turned out there was some shoot-'em-up cops and robbers show on TV on Tuesday nights. Got him all riled up.

"These fires were in the Soquel Valley. All old barns, all

within five miles of each other. Turned out to be a neighbor. Guy in his early twenties, lived with his parents. Get this: his name was Larry. Larry Rogers."

Jeri stared at Walt.

He nodded. "He's a registered arsonist."

SEVENTEEN

At ten o'clock the next morning I was down at my barn, waiting for Blue. The sky was brassy and overcast, the air heavy and humid, as it had been all week. I could feel the gathering charge in the atmosphere; when I brushed my hair, the strands crackled with static electricity.

As my body tingled with desire. It had been five days since I'd seen Blue and I wanted him.

Like electricity, like flames, the current surged along my nerves. Just the thought of Blue's touch set a pulse up the insides of my thighs.

How could it be so sudden, so complete? A month ago, Blue Winter was an interesting possibility on my horizon; today he was a presence deep in my core.

Nature's way. Even as I twirled a stem of oat hay between my fingers, Jack the rooster flapped his wings and jumped on Red's back in the ubiquitous act of passion. Red squatted to support him; in an instant, or so it seemed to me, Jack was done and off. Both chickens fluffed their feathers up and looked satisfied. Mates.

The sexual urge meant one thing in the natural world. Find a partner and procreate. I shivered suddenly as I watched the chickens peck happily in the dust, their peeping chicks spread around them. Was that what was happening here? The old biological clock catching up with me? Did I just want a mate?

Maybe I did. But, I reassured myself, this urge was particular. I didn't just want *a* mate. I wanted Blue.

Roey woofed softly by my feet. A green pickup driving in. My heart beat faster. My God, I thought. Just the sight of his truck is enough.

Blue parked and opened his door. Freckles jumped out before he did. In a moment the dogs were sniffing noses, tails wagging. Freckles wiggled all over.

I laughed. Blue met my eyes.

"There's something about that dog that makes me giggle," I told him.

"I know. World's funniest-looking dog."

"She is different."

It was an understatement. Half Jack Russell terrier, half Australian shepherd, Freckles had stiff, wiry fur that was mostly white with assorted liver-colored blotches. Her eyes were light blue; her muzzle had terrier whiskers and her tail was long, white, and plumed. She was about the silliest-looking dog I'd ever seen.

"Here, Freckles," I called.

She ran up to me to be petted, wiggled once, ran back to Roey and frisked around her. In a moment both dogs were playing tag, Roey yapping happily as she ran.

"Well, they're having fun," I said.

"How about us?"

In another moment I was in Blue's arms, my mouth pressed to his, his hands running up and down my spine. Sensations overwhelmed me—the texture of his lips, the warmth of his tongue, the firmness of his body against mine.

We broke apart and Blue smiled. "I missed you," he said.

"Me, too."

I stared into his smiling eyes, my heart thumping crazily in my chest. I wanted nothing more than to drag him into the hay barn and wrestle him to the straw.

No, Gail, my mind lectured. Don't go there. Maintain some semblance of control.

I took a deep breath. "Maybe we should work the colt first," I said.

Blue's grin grew wider. "If you want. How about one more kiss, just to keep me going?"

And then we were in each other's arms again.

So much. So much feeling rushing through me. So much wanting, so much need. It felt like a torrent, gushing through my body as I wrapped my arms around Blue's neck and pulled him down to me.

"I want you," I murmured.

"I can tell."

We both laughed, breaking apart again.

"Okay," he said. "First the horse."

"Right."

I went to the corral to catch Danny, thinking that I had never felt desire like this before. Never had I wanted any body so much. Literally any "body." My body wanted Blue Winter's body in a deep, yearning, intense way I was unprepared for.

It unnerved me somewhat. I put the halter on Danny without really seeing the horse, doing the familiar actions on automatic pilot, still wondering what in the world had come over me. It wasn't just lust; I knew that feeling; I could deal with it. This was something else, this longing to be mated.

Danny bumped my elbow with his nose as I opened the gate of his pen, as if to say, Look at me.

I stroked his neck absently as I guided him out the gate, noticing that he walked quietly, obedient to my control. A good sign.

Leading the horse up to the round pen, I asked Blue, "How is it going to work, just riding him on weekends?"

"It's not ideal," he said quietly.

"That I know. There just isn't much I can do about it right now. I haven't gotten home before dark once this week."

Blue shrugged. "You do what you can do. Just like everything else in life. In a perfect world, you'd work with this horse every

135

day, except when you felt he needed some time off. It will be harder to train him if you can only work with him on weekends. But if that's what you can do, that's what you can do."

"You're right." I sent Danny trotting around the pen, admiring his long, graceful stride as I spoke. "Anything I can do to help compensate?"

"Take a lot of time with his warm-up. Make sure he's thoroughly aired out and has all the kinks out of his legs before you try to teach him anything new. Especially before you get on him. That will give him a chance to settle down and learn."

"All right," I said.

Twenty minutes later Danny's coat was damp with sweat and his breathing was notably elevated. He'd more or less volunteered the exertion, moving freely around me with very little encouragement. I could see in his eyes that he was ready to rest.

"What do you think?" I asked Blue.

"I'd get on him right now," he said.

Without hesitation, as if it were the most natural thing in the world, I said, "Whoa" to Danny and waited until he came to a stop in front of me. I rubbed his forehead, checked to make sure his cinch was tight, took the lead rope in one hand, and climbed on him, all in one motion. The colt stood quietly, and I patted his neck.

Blue grinned from ear to ear. "That was perfect. Just like you did it every day of your life."

I grinned back at him in a rush of exhilaration. Clucking to Danny, I walked him around the pen a few times, then trotted a couple of laps. He responded obediently, completely docile, and answered my "whoa" with alacrity.

"Now what?" I asked Blue as Danny came to a stop.

"I'd quit if I were you. He's really accepting the idea of being ridden. Tomorrow we can work on bitting him up a little, maybe."

"Sounds good to me." I patted Danny's neck and slid off of him. Stroking the horse's shoulder one more time, I loosened the cinch and led him out of the pen.

Blue met me at the gate with a hug. "You done good," he said into my ear.

And then we were kissing each other again, Danny forgotten at the end of his lead rope.

"It feels so right," Blue said, when we finally separated.

It was right, I thought: This man and I together, our dogs at our heels, the shared collaboration on the colt, this place, this moment. It was right.

"You could move your trailer out here if you wanted," I said. "I mean, when you need to move."

For a long moment Blue regarded me steadily and said nothing. I couldn't read his face.

With the thought, fear rushed in. What had I said? Maybe Blue didn't feel as I did. Maybe lust struggled with claustrophobia in his heart. I'd known many men who no sooner felt entangled with a woman than they had to run. Maybe my offer sounded like a snare.

I waited. The silence went on.

"You'd be my landlady?" he said finally.

"I guess." Doubt made my voice rough. Instantly I added, "It's just an idea."

"Where would we put the trailer?" Blue was looking around.

I waved a hand. "There, by the vegetable garden, I thought."

Blue followed my gaze. "That could work, I suppose." He looked at me again. "Really?"

I nodded my head at him. "Yes. I guess."

"You don't seem too sure," he said.

"I don't know what to say." I looked at the ground. Then Blue's arms were around me. I could feel his hand tipping my chin up so my mouth met his. "Thank you," he said, "for even thinking of it."

And suddenly the doubts went flying away like departing crows. Once again I sensed the rightness, knew it was worth trying.

"Think about it," I said to Blue. "I'm sure we could work something out."

"I will," he said. "Now let's put that horse away."

* * *

Two hours later we lay in my bed, wrapped in each other's arms, Blue's steady heartbeat against my chest. Pale, milky sunlight filtered through the window; I could see the big blue gum outside, standing sentinel on the ridge. Roey and Freckles lay sacked out next to the bed, side by side.

I took a deep, happy breath. This, I thought, is what content feels like. I want nothing more.

The tree on the ridge rippled gently, its slender leaves alive to the most delicate air currents. Creamy yellow blossoms— silky, tassel-like heads—mingled with blue-silver seedpods on the crowns of the eucalyptus, shining like snow in the sun. I lay in my bed, next to my lover, staring at the big tree. Thoughts filtered in and out of my mind.

"My God," I said quietly. "I forgot to tell you. There was another fire last night."

"Oh no."

"Harkins Valley Stables. Where Lucy Kaplan trains. And it's possible a man died."

"Oh no," Blue said again. "Who?"

"A caretaker named Frank. That's all I heard."

Suddenly I was restless. Slipping out of Blue's arms, I padded naked into the other room and picked up the phone. Rummaging through my address book, I found the number I was looking for. Jeri Ward's cell phone. She'd given it to me this last summer, when we'd collaborated on another matter.

Jeri answered on the first ring. "Detective Ward."

"It's Gail McCarthy," I said. "I was thinking about the fire last night. Was the caretaker killed?"

"I'm afraid so," Jeri said. "Firefighters found him this morning. Found his bones, anyway. He must have been trying to get the horses out and got trapped in there. The fire burned most of his flesh away."

"My God," I said. "Same m.o. for the fire?"

"Walt says yes."

"And Larry Rogers?"

"We'll be taking him in for questioning this afternoon."

138

"He's sticking by his story?"

"So far. His wife confirms that he was home with her, watching TV. He admits to having set those barn fires in '85, but says he's been clean since. There's no evidence we can find to the contrary."

"Still, it's a pretty big coincidence, don't you think?"

I could hear Jeri's sigh clearly. "You wouldn't believe how often we find these weird coincidences, Gail. It's really true what they say about life being stranger than fiction. No mystery writer could get away with the freaky stuff we turn up. Larry Rogers being at these fires could be just that, a freaky coincidence."

"But you don't think so?" I asked her.

"I don't know."

"Why did he set the other fires?"

"It was a really strange deal. He lived in a part of the Soquel Valley that had a lot of horses, just like Harkins Valley. He says he thought the horses stank. He never gave any other reason for burning the barns down."

"Sounds pretty weird to me. How did he get caught that time?"

"Caught in the act while he was lighting his fifth fire. By the guy that owned the barn. I guess Larry put up something of a fight, but the owner was a tough old rodeo cowboy named Brown who beat our boy Larry up pretty thoroughly and then called 911."

"Wow," I said slowly. "Quite the story."

"Yeah, it is. Anyway, I have to go. I'm on my way to pick Larry up and take him downtown."

"Good luck," I told her.

Hanging up the phone, I returned to bed and Blue. He'd heard my half of the conversation; I filled him in on the rest.

"Damn," he said when I was done. "Sounds like they've caught the guy."

"It does," I agreed. "It sure does."

EIGHTEEN

The next night I had a date with Clay Bishop. I'd made my excuses to Blue, saying merely that I had a commitment, then called Clay and asked him out to dinner. The net result was that I was now feeling guilty for having misled both men.

It was time, I argued with myself, to straighten this out. I needed to talk to Clay, let him know I was committed to someone else, let him say what he had to say. We both needed some closure. Tomorrow I would tell Blue what I had done and that would be that.

Clay and I had agreed to meet at the old Bayview Hotel, one of my favorite dinner spots. Seated on the enclosed veranda, across a white-skirted table from a handsome, apparently self-possessed, and very quiet Clay, I found myself at a complete loss for words.

I just didn't know how to lead into it. Facing this man, I was struck by how much I genuinely liked him. From his long-lashed eyes to his understated competence and intelligence, I found him very appealing. Without Blue Winter's presence in my life, I would have been very happy to go out with Clay indefinitely.

But Blue's presence was a tangible thing, and Clay's appeal just wasn't in the same league. I needed to find the right words.

I opened my mouth to speak. What I heard coming out was, "I haven't seen you since Lucy Kaplan's fire."

"Yeah," Clay said heavily. "Poor Frank."

"Did you know him?"

"Not really. I'd met him once or twice, down at the store. He seemed like a nice old man." Clay's face looked strained. "I guess they've caught the guy who did it."

News travels fast in a small community. "Sounds like they might have," I agreed.

Clay picked somewhat gingerly at the food on his plate. "It would sure be a big relief for everyone."

"It would."

"Next Friday everybody in Harkins Valley with a boarding stable is going to be scared to death."

"They were all boarding stables, weren't they?"

"Yeah, they were. Ours first," Clay said. "Then Christy's, then Lucy's."

"You're right." I hadn't been struck by the boarding stable aspect before and wondered what it might mean. Perhaps Larry Rogers felt that there were too many big horse barns in the area. If he was true to form, maybe he thought they smelled.

I watched Clay eat his steak and tried to get myself back on track. Somehow or other, I needed to find the right words. I really did not want to hurt this man.

As if on cue, Clay met my eyes. "So what's on your mind?" he asked.

I sighed. "This isn't easy for me to say, but I need to tell you. I'm dating someone else." There. It was out. I felt a huge sense of relief.

Clay was quiet for a long moment. "I understand. We're not committed to each other yet. I was hoping you were going to tell me that you're ready to be more involved, but I can wait. I'm a patient man."

My relief evaporated at his words. "Clay, I don't think you understand. I am involved. With the other person."

Clay met my eyes steadily. "For how long?" he asked.

"A couple of weeks."

"It may not last."

"That's true. Then again, it might."

I was puzzled by Clay's reaction. Outwardly he was as calm and cool as ever, but I had the sense there was a lot going on underneath that smooth surface.

"I just wanted you to understand why I won't be dating you anymore," I went on. "It's not that I don't like you, because I do, I really do. I want you to know that."

Once again Clay's eyes held mine. "Then maybe, in the end, you'll choose me. I won't give up on you, Gail."

Now what was that supposed to mean? I stared at Clay, feeling flattered and unnerved at the same time. No one that I had dated as casually as I had Clay had ever seemed this determined. I wouldn't have said I was the type to inspire such a feeling.

But here I was, finishing my sautéed salmon over rice in front of a quiet man who had just announced his intention to keep pursuing me despite the fact that I had chosen his rival.

Once again Clay spoke as if he could intuit my thought. "You don't need to worry. I won't bother you. Or your new boyfriend. I just want you to know I'll be there. If you ever change your mind."

"All right," I said.

Something about his tone was disturbing me. The words were reasonable enough, but his face was so calm, his voice so even. It just didn't feel right. I wanted a change of subject, and quickly.

"So how are things at home?" I asked him. "How's your mom? Is Bart going to be able to rebuild the big barn?"

I knew I was babbling, but Clay took my questions as smoothly as he had taken my earlier statement.

"Mom's been tired lately. It's hard on Bart. But it does look like the insurance company is going to come through, so Bart ought to be able to build some kind of a barn."

"That's good. They'll pay in a case of arson, then."

"Apparently. As long as you're not the arsonist."

"Makes sense."

I took the last bite of my salmon just as my cell phone rang.

142

I'd warned Clay I was on call; he nodded in understanding as I excused myself and answered the phone.

It was the answering service, naturally. A colic, of course. Up in the wilds of the San Lorenzo Valley, a good hour away. I found I was actually delighted.

Saying a hasty good-bye to Clay, and leaving a fifty-dollar bill to cover the meal, I went out and got in my truck. Alone in the dark parking lot, behind the steering wheel, I heaved a deep sigh of relief.

I never would have imagined that I'd prefer a colic call to a dinner date, but Clay's reaction had been unsettling. I started the truck with an odd little frisson along my nerves. I was glad to be getting away.

Monday morning Jim was back at work. Closeted in his office an hour before anyone else was due in, I was relieved, exasperated, and apologetic, all in turns.

"The thing is," I said, "nothing I do seems to help. The guy is determined to hate me."

I was overstating the case, probably. But then, I'd had a month of John Romero's sulkiness to deal with on my own. Who could blame me for dramatizing the situation a little?

Jim, apparently. "We need him, Gail. Can't you just manage to get along with him?"

This was a predictable reaction. Jim wasn't interested in dealing with emotional issues on the part of his employees. However, I was no longer merely an employee.

"Maybe we could find someone else. Someone I could get along with. Or maybe Hans Schmidt is going to steal enough of our business that we won't need a third vet."

"I don't think so." Jim gave me a hard-edged glance. "Hans Schmidt won't be stealing our business for long."

"Why's that?"

"I know Hans from way back and he's no horse vet. He doesn't know jack about horses."

"You're kidding."

"Nope. Hans is strictly a small animal vet. Practiced for years up in San Francisco. His daughter's the one who's into horses. She got him down here, encouraged him to expand his business into large animals, too. But he's really afraid of horses. People will notice after awhile. Horse owners aren't dumb." Jim laughed, a short, sharp bark. "Once the women get over being charmed by him, anyway."

"You really think he's afraid of horses?"

"Hell, yes. He practically knocks one out just to float its teeth. He won't do any sort of work on any horse, no matter how gentle, without sedating it until it's staggering."

"Is that right?"

I was surprised, but I knew better than to disbelieve. Jim might be a hard-driving dynamo of a boss, with very little sympathy for his employees' personal problems, but he was a deeply knowledgeable vet, and his harsh assessment of another veterinarian was likely to be accurate. I'd known Jim for many years now; he was seldom wrong. Often rude, perhaps, but usually right.

"Hans Schmidt will be lucky to stay out of jail, anyway," Jim added grimly. "That'll take care of our problem."

"What do you mean?"

"All that animal rights stuff he's involved in. It landed him in jail before. A few years ago. I forget exactly why. Ask him; he'll probably tell you. He's proud of it." Jim rubbed his close-shaven jaw with its deep dimple, his short, stubby fingers clean and callused. "I think he burned a barn down or something."

"What?" I must have sounded as shocked as I felt, because Jim's eyes whipped to my face.

"Yeah, a barn, or maybe it was a laboratory. I can't remember. Somewhere that animals were 'held captive,' anyway. You know the rhetoric."

"I sure do. Hans has spouted it at me himself, many a time. But Jim, I guess you don't know, since you've been gone." And I told him about the arsonist in Harkins Valley.

"Wow," he said. "That's hard to believe. But you say they've caught the guy."

144

"They've got a guy, yeah. And he seems like an obvious candidate. He's been at all these fires; I've seen him, just staring like he was completely enthralled. It's creepy. But hell, Hans has been at all these fires, too. And I'm pretty sure the fire investigator and the detective don't know he has a record of arson."

"Well, he wouldn't advertise it under the circumstances, would he?"

"No," I agreed.

"Unfortunately, I don't think this sounds like Hans and his buddies. Wouldn't they leave large notices that the barns were burned in order to free the animals? Much as I'd enjoy seeing him behind bars," Jim added.

"I don't know," I said. "Hans is getting some benefit out of these fires, himself. Or his daughter is. Some of the horses in the barns that burned have been moved to Quail Run Ranch."

"Oh-ho," Jim grinned his brief, triangular grin.

"Right," I said. "I wonder."

We stared at each other for a moment. Jim shrugged. "Try to get along with John," was all he said. Then he was out the door.

"Right," I said again to the empty air.

NINETEEN

$\mathbf{M}$y week progressed as my weeks usually did. Busy. Damn busy. I found no opportunities to talk to John, not that it would necessarily have helped if I had, judging by my last attempt. The man was clearly avoiding me, anyway.

Neither did I find an opportunity to see Blue. We were both working hard and getting in late—no time or energy for dinner dates or their aftermath. Most nights he called me, though. We talked about the weekend.

I thought about the weekend—a lot. And I thought about Friday night. I had the urge to call Jeri and ask how the investigation was progressing, but I resisted.

Reminding myself that it wasn't my business, and I did have plenty of business of my own, I kept my curious fingers off the phone. But I wondered. I wondered a lot. I listed the other boarding stables in Harkins Valley off in my mind. There were at least half a dozen of them. I wondered if Jeri would consider mounting some kind of guard.

If I could think of this sort of thing, so would she, I reminded myself. It was hardly rocket science, more like adding two plus two and getting four.

Friday morning did not begin auspiciously, at least for me.

My first call was to a jumping horse who was suffering from a mysterious lameness, "somewhere high in the rear end." Oh no, I thought, when Nancy gave me the word. These were always the hardest sorts of lameness to diagnose.

This case didn't turn out to be any easier than I'd expected. The horse was a ten-year-old chestnut gelding named Reddy, a good and useful hunter over fences. His owner, a woman in her twenties, reported that the horse had seemed to her to be "moving funny behind," but she could detect no obvious lameness. Then, yesterday, he'd fallen with her while jumping a two-and-a-half-foot fence.

"I'm all right," she said, wincing and rubbing her left shoulder. "But there's definitely something wrong with him. He's never fallen before, and he can jump twice that height. Easily."

"All right," I said. "Let's jog him in a few circles."

Reddy knew how to longe and he trotted freely around us in both directions at the end of a long line. As his owner had said, he had no easily detectable lameness, but he did seem to be moving his hind legs stiffly.

I watched him for several minutes and then sighed. "This is a hard one," I told the woman frankly. "I'll do the spavin test on him, just to make sure, but I think his hocks are fine. He's not stifled, and he doesn't appear to have a dropped hip. Other possibilities are his back, particularly the sacroiliac joint, or some kind of pulled muscle in his rump. Or it could be a disease called EPM that's caused by a parasite."

The woman shook her head, looking as baffled as I felt. "So, where do we start?"

"Spavin test and some blood work, to see if it's EPM," I said. "Confine him in a small pen or stall and give him complete rest for a couple of weeks, in case it's a muscle or a back thing. By the way," I asked her, "is there any possibility it's the result of a traumatic injury?"

She shook her head. "Not that I know of. He fell with me after he started doing this."

"Does he pull back?" I asked.

"Yeah, he does from time to time." We looked at each other,

and I saw the proverbial lightbulb click on behind her eyes. "You know, he pulled back real hard, less than a month ago. He was tied to the trailer when I was at a show and something scared him, I'm not sure what. I saw him pull back, though. He was tied solid and he sat back on the lead rope as hard as he could for a full minute."

"What happened?" I asked her.

"The lead rope broke and he went over backward," she said. "He got right up and seemed fine, so I never thought about it again. But . . ."

"That could have done it," I said. "Horses can hurt their spinal cords that way."

"If that's the cause," she asked, "what's the diagnosis?"

"I'm not sure," I said honestly. "Back injury, to be glib. Just like in humans, backs are difficult to diagnose. I'd give him two weeks' complete rest, and if he's not better we may need to x-ray his back. We'll have to sedate him for that and lay him out flat; it's not an easy procedure with a horse. Another possibility is a chiropractor."

"They have those for horses?" She laughed.

"Yeah, they sure do. And acupuncturists and homeopathic practitioners, too. I can give you the names of a couple of equine chiropractors who have good reputations," I said.

"Do you believe in that stuff?"

"I don't know enough about it to make a judgment," I told her. "I have seen some horses with chronic problems that did seem to get better under some of these alternative therapies. Those horses might have gotten better anyway, I don't know. But if I had a horse with an obscure back problem, I'd probably consult both a chiropractor and an acupuncturist before I tried anything too invasive in the way of Western medicine."

"Really?"

"Sure, Western medicine is great for acute conditions; it has no peer, in my opinion. But long-term chronic conditions can be problematic. Allergies, back pain, that sort of thing. I think alternative therapies are definitely worth looking at there."

"All right. I'll consider that."

I finished up my exam, drew some blood, and gave the woman the numbers of the two equine chiropractors I thought well of. My cell phone rang as she was writing them down.

"Judith Rainier has a colic," Nancy said. "Can you go?"

"I can leave right now," I said. "Tell her I'll be there in twenty minutes."

Taking my leave of Reddy and his owner, I headed for Harkins Valley and Judith's place. Sandwiched between two fancy horse operations, the Rainier family ranch was decidedly humble in comparison. Both the old barn and the little house looked worn down and weary, and the pastures were fenced with sagging strands of less-than-desirable barbed wire fence. The whole place had the look of one that nobody had put any money into for twenty years.

This might be true, as far as I knew. Judith had inherited the place from her parents long ago, and I didn't think she had any spare cash to use on ranch improvements. A single mom with two daughters, she held down a full-time job and seemed to put most of her income into her children's various horsey pursuits.

I drove along the narrow, bumpy, deeply rutted driveway to find Judith and her daughters waiting for me out at the barn.

"It's Mabel. She's colicked," the older one said, as I got out of the cab.

I knew the two girls apart by sight, but could never remember their names. The older daughter had a long blond braid and was deeply attached to her horses. However, I couldn't remember who Mabel was. I looked to Judith for enlightenment.

"Jamie's old barrel racing horse," Judith said. "She's twenty-two. We found her out in the field this morning, lying down. We think she's colicked."

"Let's go have a look," I said.

Following the girls out through a wire gate, I noticed at least a dozen horses peering over the fences at us.

"Are these all yours?" I asked Judith.

"No. I board some for the girls' friends. Some of these kids are really into high school rodeo, but they live in town and have no place to keep a horse. So I keep their horses out here. It brings in a little income, and that way they can practice here in our arena with Jamie and Jodie."

"What events do you do?" I asked the girls.

"Barrels and goat tying," they answered. Almost in unison.

"We've got a rodeo this evening in Merced," the younger one added.

Jamie pointed to a horse lying flat on its side ahead of us. "Oh my God," she said. "Is she dead?"

She wasn't. The horse lifted her head as we approached, then got to her feet. Snorting, she pawed the ground twice and settled back down on her belly.

"Looks like a colic to me," I said. "Let's check her out."

Jamie caught the mare, who was a pale, creamy color, like buttermilk. Technically a palomino, Mabel was what most western horsemen describe as a "yellow" horse. Plain headed, with no withers to speak of and a round, barrel-shaped look to her, she was not what I would call a prepossessing animal.

Judith caught my expression and smiled. "I know she doesn't look like much, but she was actually a great barrel horse. Jamie won a lot on her. She was competitive until she was twenty, too."

"What stopped her?" I asked, as I checked the mare's vital signs.

Judith pointed at the mare's right front foot. "Ringbone," she said succinctly.

I could see the calcified joint easily. Ringbone, an arthritic condition of the pastern joint, was almost always crippling in the end.

Finishing my exam, I said, "She seems to have some sort of mild to moderate colic going on. Her pulse and respiration are elevated, but not a lot, and she has some gut sounds. Again, not a lot. She clearly has some distress. I'll give her some painkillers and pump some mineral oil into her, and we'll see how she does.

"Keep a good eye on her. The painkillers will wear off in about four to six hours. If she shows signs of getting painful again, I ought to have a look at her."

"That's the problem," Judith said, with a worried look on her face. Both the girls looked miserable.

"What's that?" I asked.

"We need to leave at noon to get to Merced on time," Judith answered, looking at her watch. "That's one hour from now. I wasn't planning to be home until tomorrow night. I don't know what to do about this horse."

"Can you have someone else check on her?" I asked.

"Everybody's going," Judith said simply. "I'm hauling six horses and six teenagers. One of the kids' moms will be hauling another four horses and two more girls. All that will be left here is this old mare and one other retired gelding."

Jamie was stroking the yellow mare's neck, tears running quietly down her face.

"Hey, it's not a problem," I told her. "I'll come back here later and have a look at your horse."

It was more than worth it to see her face light up.

"Gail," Judith said dubiously, "I appreciate your offering, but this horse is just a pet now. I don't mind paying for one call, but I'm not sure about two."

"That's okay," I said. "This will be on my time. I have some scheduled calls in the south county this afternoon, and I'll just stop here on my way home. It's right on my way. No trouble." I smiled at Jamie. "I'll take good care of her. Don't worry."

Jamie smiled back at me, a little tremulously.

"Do you think she'll be okay?" she asked.

"I think so," I said honestly. "She doesn't seem to be that badly colicked. Of course, you never know."

"I know," Jamie said quietly. "And thank you."

"You're welcome," I told her.

"I really appreciate this," Judith added, as we all walked back out to my truck.

"No problem." I smiled at Jamie. "Win the barrel race for me."

And then I was on the way to my next call, a prepurchase soundness exam in San Juan Bautista. This was followed by a sole abscess in Salinas, quite a bit south of my usual territory, but the woman was a loyal client who had moved. A puncture wound, an eye injury, and a bowed tendon completed my day, or so I thought.

Nancy called me at six o'clock as I was driving toward home. "I've got a horse in Aromas who caught his leg between two pipe panels and was hung up there. The owner found him that way when she got home. His pastern is cut very deeply, he's really bleeding."

"I'll head on out there," I told her, knowing that Jim had been completely booked up since he got back. And I was not, I was damn well not, going to ask John Romero for any more favors.

Aromas was half an hour south of me, and the cut turned out to be a bad one. It was eight o'clock and black-dark by the time I finished the stitching. Eager to get home, I jumped on the freeway, only to recall my promise to Jamie Rainier.

"Damn," I said out loud.

Not only was one more call the last thing I wanted, but I had really left the old mare unchecked for much longer than I'd intended. I hoped she would be fine.

I took the first exit I came to, and headed inland to Harkins Valley, my mind fixed on getting through this errand as quickly as possible. I wanted food and rest and a glass of wine, not necessarily in that order.

Judith Rainier's place was dark and quiet, as I expected. Grabbing my flashlight, a halter, and my stethoscope, I hopped out of my truck and went to look for Mabel. Fortunately, her light color made her easy to spot in the dark, and I found her right away.

She looked fine, I was relieved to see, and a quick check showed that all vital signs were normal. Good enough.

Pulling the wire gate to the pasture closed behind me, I was headed for my truck at a brisk clip when I slowed to a stop, halted by a sense of something not right.

What? I scanned. Judith's house lay quiet under the night sky; an owl hooted softly in the big oak in her barnyard. The barn was silent, too, and the shed beyond. But . . .

I froze and my eyes scooted back to the barn. I'd caught it on the periphery of my vision—light. Light in the barn, and not electric lights either. This was the faint, orangy flickering glow of firelight.

I stared at the black square that was the big open doorway in the center of the barn. It was there. Barely perceptible, but there. As if, I caught my breath, there was candlelight somewhere deep inside.

Candlelight. Candles. Shit. In a rush I remembered the arsonist and all the speculation that the work day had driven out of my mind.

In a second I'd shifted direction from my truck to the barn. Damn. Maybe I'd catch the arsonist myself. At the thought, I paused. I had no weapon, unless I counted that heavy metal flashlight in my hand, which might double as a billy club in an emergency. Still, I did have something.

I dug my phone out of my pocket and dialed Jeri Ward's cell, thanking God I had a good memory for numbers, phone numbers in particular.

Jeri answered on the first ring. "Ward here."

"Jeri, this is Gail McCarthy. Where are you?"

"Cruising down Harkins Valley Road, looking for trouble. Why?"

"I'm at 2620 Harkins Valley," I said. "Judith Rainier's place. I was checking on a colic. No one's home and I think I see firelight in the barn."

"We'll be right there," Jeri affirmed.

"Okay."

"Gail," Jeri said, "wait where you are."

"Right," I said, and hung up.

Staring at the barn, I gave a moment's thought to this course of action. The flickering light deep within the doorway seemed to grow brighter as I watched. Shit. I was not going to stand here waiting while Judith's barn caught on fire. Gripping the flashlight in my right hand, I headed for the doorway.

Like many old barns, the central cavity beyond the big open double doors was large and airy, meant for hay storage. I could see the quavering glow deep within; all else was blackness. I clicked my flashlight on.

Swinging the beam about, I saw a haystack in front of me, box stalls along the sides, it looked like. And alongside the stack of baled hay were half a dozen candles, surrounded by chaff and crumpled papers.

I stared. The candles flickered and guttered, looking fragile and insubstantial in the dark night. Nothing else was burning, yet.

Stepping through the doorway, I moved toward the tiny merciless flames. In that moment I heard a rustle to my right. I turned in that direction and blackness came rushing in.

TWENTY

I came to slowly, like a fish swimming up through dark water. Concerned faces peered down at me as I rose to the surface. Strangers' faces. Male. I stared blankly at them with a rush of fear.

Who were these people? Who was I? Tears rose up in my eyes and rolled down my cheeks.

A female face joined the male ones. Blond hair, somehow familiar. I could feel a warm hand holding mine.

"Gail. It's Jeri," the voice said.

Slowly, slowly, it seemed, memory returned. I was a vet; I was here on a call. This was Jeri Ward. My head pounded with pain.

"What happened?" I asked.

"Someone hit you over the head," Jeri answered. "The arsonist, we think. Did you see him?"

I closed my eyes. The pounding pain in my head was getting worse.

"I don't remember," I said slowly. I could hear sirens wailing in the background.

"Don't worry," Jeri said. "The ambulance is here. They'll take you to the hospital; we'll get you checked out. I think you have a concussion. Do you want me to call anyone?"

"No," I said dully.

"I'll be down there as soon as I'm done here," she said. "I'll drive you home, if they'll let you go, and I'll have one of the boys bring your truck home."

"Thanks." There were more faces now. Firm hands were loading me onto a stretcher. I felt passive, an inert bundle. My head hurt.

My first-ever ambulance ride passed in a blur. I was aware of machines and lights, reassuring voices, strangers in charge. I lay on my back and let go. Events had gone beyond my control. The throbbing pain inside my head was my only concern.

I arrived at the emergency room of the hospital in a way that reminded me of baggage at an airport. Attendants carried me inside and decanted me, gently and professionally, onto a hospital bed. A curtain was drawn around me; medical professionals checked on my well-being and assured me that a doctor would see me soon.

I waited. My head pounded. After what seemed to me a good long while, I asked for painkillers and was told a doctor would have to prescribe them. I was reassured that said doctor would be here soon.

It wasn't soon, but eventually a doctor did appear. Indian or Pakistani, by the look of her, her nametag proclaimed her as one Gita Smith. She examined me quickly and competently, told me I had a concussion, ordered a CAT scan, and wrote me a prescription for pain pills.

"Can I go?" I asked.

"If that CAT scan shows nothing amiss," she agreed.

An hour later, the CAT scan confirming me as relatively normal, merely concussed, Dr. Smith told me I could leave. "If you have someone to drive you home and stay with you. You should not be alone."

"Right," I agreed, though I hadn't the faintest idea how I would manage this. The pain pills had diminished my headache considerably, but I felt as though I was operating in a fog.

156

As I was struggling to come up with some kind of coherent plan, Jeri Ward made an appearance. Brushing into my curtained cubicle with the brisk assurance of a policewoman, she assured the medical minions that she, Detective Jeri Ward, would take personal responsibility for Dr. McCarthy.

I watched her manage my exit from the hospital and marveled at her appearance. Despite the fact that it was well after midnight and her evening had no doubt been nearly as stressful as mine, she looked amazingly clean, neat, and elegant, in a flax-colored linen suit that was as miraculously unwrinkled as her wavy blond hair was crisp and unmussed.

Just how did she do that? I looked relatively disheveled an hour after I'd combed my hair and dressed myself, even if I was only sitting in an armchair, reading a book.

Jeri's actions were as deft and polished as her appearance. In five minutes or less, I was loaded into a wheelchair and rolled out of the bustling confines of the emergency room and into the dark parking lot, Jeri at the helm and a hospital orderly trotting alongside.

Once I'd been helped into the passenger side of the sheriff's sedan, Jeri dismissed the orderly and climbed into the driver's seat. Shutting the door behind her, she gave me a long look.

"How are you?"

"Groggy," I said. "Like I've had one too many drinks. And my head still hurts. Though whatever they gave me made it better. What happened?"

Jeri started the car. "What do you remember?"

"I've been thinking about it," I said slowly. "My mind doesn't seem to be working too well, but I remember I was out at Judith's place to check on her daughter's old mare, who had colicked this morning. The mare was fine; I remember that.

"Then, I think, I saw light in the barn, what looked like fire-light. And I called you, right?"

"Right," Jeri confirmed, her eyes on the road.

"The rest is pretty vague. I think I walked into the barn, though I don't really remember doing it. After that, there's nothing."

"You don't remember seeing anything?"

"No." I spread my hands in frustration. "I don't even remember stepping through the doorway. Where did you find me?"

"About twenty feet inside the barn."

"So I must have gone in."

"Yes, your footprints indicate that. And there's no indication that you were moved."

"So, what happened?" I asked again.

Jeri sighed. "I got your call at eight-thirty when I was on Harkins Valley Road, less than two miles from the Rainier place. We were pulling in the driveway, lights flashing, sirens going, about five minutes after I spoke to you.

"I jumped out of the car and ran straight to the barn; there you were, lying on the ground, no sign of the arsonist. But there were a dozen lit candles with little piles of hay and paper around them. Do you remember that?"

"No," I said.

"You must have seen the candles, though, judging by where you were lying. We think the arsonist must have hit you over the head, just as we were pulling in the driveway. Then he ran."

"On foot?"

"Yes. Apparently he came and went on foot. There's no sign he used any other mode of transportation. By the time we sorted out what was going on, he was long gone. Tomorrow we'll look for tracks."

"Uh-huh." I was thinking about it, in my foggy way. "I wonder if he would have killed me," I said. "If he hadn't heard you coming."

Jeri said nothing. We drove in silence for a while. I found the dark and quiet soothing; the background pain in my head seemed to ease.

In another minute Jeri was pulling into my driveway. The sight of my corral fences in the headlights reminded me of my responsibilities.

"The horses haven't been fed," I said. "Or the dog or cat."

"Not to worry," Jeri said. "I'll take care of it."

She fed by the car's headlights, following my directions. Once the animals were all taken care of, I allowed her to escort me into the house, Roey in our wake. As soon as she'd helped me into bed, Jeri brought me the phone.

"Who shall I call to come stay with you?" she asked. "I'd stay myself, but I can't. Things are hopping. This arson case is now a big, big deal."

I closed my eyes. "You don't need to call anyone," I said. "I'll be fine. Just put the pain pills and the phone where I can reach them."

"Bullshit," said Jeri succinctly. "Someone needs to be with you. Now who?"

"There isn't anyone," I murmured. "My best friend moved away a month ago. I don't have any family." Even in my befuddled state, I was aware of how pathetic it sounded. "I guess there's my new boyfriend, but I don't want to call him at two in the morning."

Jeri gave me a look. "Gail, trust me on this one. If the guy is worth keeping, he'd be very upset if you didn't call under these circumstances."

"Oh, all right." I didn't feel up to arguing and recited the number. In another minute Jeri was talking to what I assumed was a very sleepy Blue.

The conversation didn't take long. Hanging up the phone, Jeri said with satisfaction, "He'll be right here."

"What," I said with my eyes closed, "about Larry Rogers?"

"No go," Jeri said. "I had him watched tonight. Detective parked across the street from his house confirms he was home all evening. And Marty Martin's got an even better alibi. He and his parents were with his therapist from eight until nine. Those two are out on this one."

"I suppose we assume it's been the same person all along."

"We think it's probable. Think, Gail. Who else was at all three of the fires?"

I thought. Or rather, I tried to think. The wheels just weren't turning very smoothly in my head. I felt like I was in the grip of the world's worst hangover.

"Well, Clay and Bart Bishop," I said. "No, that's not right.

Bart wasn't at the second fire; he was out on a date. But Clay was at all three. And quite a few of the horse people from Lushmeadows were there. I just don't specifically remember who was at all three."

"Who would you guess?"

"Tony Sanchez, I think. George Corfios. Warren White. I'm not sure of any others."

"Who else?"

"Well, me of course." I stopped, my foggy mind freezing up as I remembered my conversation with Jim. "And my fellow horse vets," I added slowly.

"That's right. John Romero and Hans Schmidt."

"I think," I said carefully, "you should check their records."

"Why?"

"Just check them," I said. "I heard some gossip. I don't like to repeat it; it feels like slandering someone. If it turns out to be true, I'll talk to you about it."

"All right," Jeri said.

Inwardly, my punch-drunk mind was reeling. Was it possible that Hans, courtly, silver-haired, flirtatious Hans, had hit me over the head? It seemed completely impossible. But then, everything about this situation seemed bizarre to me.

Here I lay, propped up by pillows in my familiar bed, in my small room. There in front of me, just visible in the dim light from the hall, was the carved antique dresser I'd inherited from my parents, the dresser I'd faithfully lugged from temporary home to temporary home. This was my place; this was my secure nest.

But next to me sat Detective Jeri Ward, watchful and sharp, trying to figure out who had bashed me over the head. Even through the fuzzy haze of unreality that my concussion had created, Jeri Ward shone hard and true. It had happened. Someone had attacked me.

Roey's sudden *woof* caused both Jeri and me to start. Looking out the window, I could see headlights coming up the drive.

In another second, the instant ripple of fear along my nerves had subsided, to be replaced by a glow of relief.

"Blue's here," I said, and smiled.

TWENTY-ONE

I found Blue's physical presence supremely comforting. For the rest of the night, I pressed my body against his long, warm length, as he held me in his arms. From time to time I shivered uncontrollably, though I wasn't really cold.

"It's just your body letting go of trauma," Blue murmured into my hair. "Don't fight it. It's healthy."

I cried, too: quiet, forlorn tears that ran down my cheek and dripped onto Blue's chest. Gently, he stroked my face with one finger and told me to go ahead and cry.

"It's okay," he said. "It's natural, after what you've been through."

Bit by bit, I felt my tense muscles relaxing. My jaw loosened, though I'd been unaware of holding it clenched. Slowly, slowly, I let go of some tightly knotted fist in my core. I was safe.

Despite my tiredness, I never really slept, except in fitful snatches. The pain in my head kept me awake, even through the numbing of pain pills. I could relax my body, but my head was caught in some sort of viselike pressure that wouldn't let up.

"Don't worry," Blue told me, as dawn began to lighten the eastern sky. "Concussions are like this. I've had a few myself. When I was fighting in the ring."

"You used to box?"

"In my misspent youth." He laughed. "Pretty soon you'll know all my secrets."

"There doesn't seem to be any end to the adventures you've had."

I could feel Blue's shoulder shrug slightly under my cheek.

"What an interesting life," I said softly.

Lying in his arms as the dawn sky turned to sapphire outside the window, I was aware of how much I admired Blue's past. More than anyone I'd ever met before, he seemed to have put his whole heart into following his particular dreams. Somehow or other, I was sure that his present serenity was in some sense the result of that journey.

Blue ran a hand down my leg and laughed, a deep, reassuring chuckle. "I've done a lot of things," he admitted. "When I was younger, I always wanted the words 'he tried' carved on my tombstone."

"And now?"

"And now I don't care what's on my tombstone." I could hear the smile in Blue's voice. "I only care what's in my heart."

I sighed, snuggled deeper into his arms, and closed my eyes.

I must have slept, finally, because when I opened my eyes again bright sunlight was streaming in the window. I couldn't see Blue, but I could smell coffee.

After a minute I started to climb out of bed, but ended up sitting on the edge of the mattress as a wave of dizziness washed over me. My head still ached, and disconcertingly, there was a constant ringing buzz in my ears.

In another second Blue stood in the bedroom doorway. "I thought I heard you moving around. How do you feel?"

"Like shit." I stared up at Blue. "How long is this going to last?"

"Hard to say." He sat down on the bed next to me. "In my experience, concussions are unpredictable. The symptoms can last a long time, or they can go away quickly."

"What's a long time?" I reached for the pain pills as I said it.

"Well, I knew one guy where they lasted for months," Blue said reluctantly.

"Months!" I almost dropped the plastic vial of tablets. "Shit. How am I going to work like this?"

Blue put an arm around my shoulder. "One step at a time, Stormy. Let's just see how today goes."

I swallowed a couple of pills and put my hand on Blue's thigh. "All right. I know you're right."

"How about a cup of coffee?"

"Sounds good to me."

Blue plied me with coffee and toast and massaged my aching head until the pills kicked in. I found he'd also fed the horses and washed the dirty dishes that were piled in my sink.

"Thank you," I said awkwardly, somewhat embarrassed.

"It's not a problem. I can take care of you, Stormy."

I stared at him, sitting in a waterfall of sunlight that poured in the big windows; red-gold sparks seemed to cling to the fine hairs on his forearm. Even a year ago the notion of a man presuming to take care of me would have been unwelcome and upsetting. Today I found myself comforted by his words.

In fact, I realized, I very much wanted Blue Winter's presence here in my house; I wanted his protection; I wanted his caring. In every sense that I understood wanting a man, I wanted Blue. As a mate.

Mate. At the word, I smiled. I seemed to be doing a lot of thinking about mates lately. Must be the old biological clock.

"In Australia, people call their friends 'mates,' don't they?" I asked Blue idly.

"They do." Blue smiled at me across the table. "Are you my mate?"

"Could be," I said. "What do you think?"

"We're working on it."

"Yeah." I hesitated. "Is that all right with you?"

Blue's turn to hesitate. When he spoke, it was in formal tones. "I think so. How about you?"

I sighed. "I don't know if I should say this, but yes. I'm

163

seriously thinking of asking you to move your trailer out here. I'll make you a deal on rent you can't refuse."

Blue smiled. "What would that be?"

"You can pay me in kisses."

He laughed.

"Or whatever you want."

"All right." Blue was suddenly serious. "We can try it if you want. We'll end up living together, you know."

"I know." I smiled at him.

"It might," he said carefully, "be a strain on our relationship, me moving in so soon."

"I know," I said again. "But I'm willing to try."

Blue grinned at me. "Well, it was always my motto."

"I have to warn you," I said, "I've never lived with anyone before. This will be a first."

"Well, I've lived with three different women. And though there were different problems, in some ways it was the same, if you know what I mean. The proximity of living together does something to a relationship. It takes some of the mystery out of it. Are you ready for that?"

"I think so." I looked at him. "What I think is that a relationship is like a garden. It requires constant tending. Some seasons not much needs to be done, others there will be lots of work. But always you need to remain aware of it and in touch with it. It's always changing and its needs won't be the same from one season to the next."

Blue met my eyes. "Tending a garden," he said. "We can do that."

I smiled. "Of course, there are a lot of weeds in my vegetable garden at this very moment."

"I can help with that."

"And what about poor Danny? I don't think I'll be working with him if my head goes on feeling like this."

I got to my feet, a little gingerly. The room didn't spin, but I had the feeling it might. Though the pills had softened my headache, they'd done nothing at all for the buzzing in my ears or the dizziness.

Blue stood up and put out a hand to me. "I can help with the colt, too. Just tell me what you want."

Stepping forward, I put my arms around Blue's waist and pressed my face into his chest. "You're too good to be true," I murmured.

Blue rested his chin on the top of my head. "Wait and see," he said. "I'm like your colt. We might look good to you now, but only time will tell how we work out in the long run."

"I'll take my chances," I said to his breastbone. "On both of you."

TWENTY-TWO

True to his word, Blue worked Danny while I watched, then weeded the vegetable garden. After that he headed back to the rose farm to tend his young plants, promising to be back by dinnertime, pizza in hand.

As his truck disappeared around the bend in the drive, I felt oddly bereft, a feeling which was rapidly replaced by an equally unfamiliar anxiety. Sitting on my front porch, overlooking my garden, I was restless and nervous, as if there were something I needed to do, something I'd forgotten.

What is this, I asked myself. I tried to sit quietly and be with the feeling, but the restlessness wouldn't let me alone. My ears buzzed; my head ached. Worst of all, the whole world looked slightly skewed.

It was nothing obvious, nothing readily identifiable. Still, the familiar blue gum tree was a stranger, I stared at my glowing scarlet begonia as if I'd never seen it before.

Taking a deep breath, I closed my eyes. My perceptions had been knocked awry and there was no knowing how long this feeling would last. I would just have to accept it and try to live with it.

Closing my eyes was a mistake. The slight sense of dizziness

I felt increased sharply, and my head spun. After a minute I stood up. Maybe I'd go for a little walk around the garden.

Slowly, clutching the porch railing with one hand, I made my way down the steps, for all the world like an old, crippled woman. Once on relatively level ground, I tried to focus on what was in front of me.

Walking around the garden was always my favorite means of relaxation. I liked to look at the plants, carefully and quietly, see how they were growing and changing. And since my garden nestled in a hollow of the wild and brushy coastal hills, I also saw a wide spectrum of animals—everything from bobcats to buzzards.

Now, step by step, I meandered along the border, trying to let my attention rest on what was there, trying to let go of this nagging edginess.

I smiled at a tall stalk of evening primrose, already gone to seed, decorated with half a dozen brilliantly yellow goldfinches, as vivid as the plant's own blooms had been in the summer. I had a love-hate relationship with evening primrose. I did not much care for its gawky shape, big, floppy leaves, or the sharp yellow of its flowers, but I loved the fact that hummingbirds visited the blooms and goldfinches, which my mother had also loved and called wild canaries, fed on the seeds.

Chickadees liked the seeds, too. I heard impudent chirps from the small, masked birds, who held their ground as I approached, fluttering away at the last minute. Chickadees were surprisingly unafraid of people. Last summer one had alighted briefly on my head.

Another few steps along the border and I stood in front of a big salvia plant called Limelight. The plant glowed as if illuminated by neon, its flowers a striking contrast between chartreuse-green bracts and indigo-blue blooms. In the early-afternoon sunlight they seemed unnaturally bright, or perhaps it was just the fragile state of my head.

On I went, staring at plants. A cottontail rabbit hopped into the border ahead of me, and a hummingbird swooped by, missing me by inches. After a moment, the little bird dive-bombed me again, then hovered briefly in front of my eyes in a show of territorial aggression. I could hear the goldfinches calling in the brush, a peculiar melancholic, three-note descending melody, a song they only sang in the fall.

Everywhere, Nature's ways were there to be read, and yet they remained mysterious. What did the goldfinches sing in the fall? Why did the hummingbird perceive me as a threat he could potentially vanquish? At the thought, a sudden crackling in the brush froze me. That had been near, very near. And by the sound of branches breaking, something large.

I stood perfectly still and scanned the brushy slope next to me, my heart pounding. Fear rushed in, all my free-floating anxiety seeming to coalesce in one surge. Who was out there?

Another second, and I saw the movement, maybe twenty feet away. Light brown hair with a sheen, moving in a gap; another stick cracked and snapped. I took a deep breath. Deer.

With more noisy rustling, the animal moved into a clearing where I could see him. A buck—a big one. In fact, I drew in my breath again, perhaps the biggest buck I'd ever seen out here.

This one was a six-pointer, and he carried his rack with a certain careful pride, in the way of older bucks. Standing there, he met my eyes as I stared. His expression was watchful but not unduly frightened. Deer who lived in these hills were used to people, and hunting was illegal. Bucks, especially, tended to have that look of wary dignity.

For my part, I watched the big animal cautiously and respectfully. In general, deer were timid creatures, but bucks could be aggressive, especially in the midst of the fall rut. This guy seemed quiet and calm, but last year an excited, snorting buck had charged in my direction. I'd avoided him easily but it wasn't an incident I'd ever forget. I hadn't known whether he'd been fighting with his fellows or run by dogs—either seemed possible—but I knew better than to assume that a buck was as docile as a bunny rabbit.

This buck and I stared at each other awhile. After a minute, he lowered his head to nibble on a vine. A rose vine, I realized. The extra-vigorous, bronzy gold climbing rose named Maigold had thrown many exploring arms up into the brush, and the buck was working on one of these. Maigold's vigor did it no good, because it was also, apparently, extra delicious; deer seemed to prefer it over any other rose I had.

I watched the buck eat my rose and reflected that all in all, it was not a bad deal. This buck was as beautiful as any plant in my garden and I was grateful to be looking at him. I studied the very black, shiny nose, the white tail and cream-colored belly, observed the delicate way he lifted his long, slender legs to step over branches. Until Roey got wind of him.

Incarcerated in her pen, the dog was no threat, but she sent a volley of barks rolling out at the animal who had invaded her yard. The buck raised his head, snorted, and departed rapidly up the ridge in a series of great bounding leaps.

Curiously, I made my way through the brush to the clearing where the deer had stood, wanting to see the size of his tracks. By my reckoning he was a very big buck for these parts.

Hunched over, I peered at the ground. My head spun. I blinked, and the dizziness cleared. I saw the buck's track in the sand. Next to it—I sucked in my breath. Sharp and clear in the loose ground—a man's footprint. Very fresh.

I froze. Thoughts tumbled. My heart began to thump and accelerated rapidly. There was no way this footprint should be here.

There was simply no possible explanation. This was my land; I had no neighbors who would trespass here. The print was an adult's foot, not a child's. And no one would go traipsing through the brush when my graveled drive was twenty feet away. There was no reason to do it. Unless the person were hiding.

I stared at the footprint. One glance told me there was no point in trying to follow tracks. The thick understory of the brush was carpeted with dry leaves; such a surface would be much beyond my limited tracking skills.

More than that, the last thing I wanted was to find the author of this footprint. I had an immediate certainty that the man who had crouched here, hidden in the brush where he could see my house, had meant me harm.

Swallowing, I made my way back to the driveway, my heart

beating so hard it almost drowned out the buzz in my ears. Walking very slowly, I searched the surrounding hills with my eyes, looking for color or motion, listening for sounds. Anything inappropriate, anything that shouldn't be there. I could find nothing, but the brush, usually so friendly and familiar, seemed threatening. The thick scrub could hide a dozen enemies.

Letting Roey out of her pen, I called her to me and shut myself in the house. For the first time in my tenure, I locked the doors. Then I got my gun out of its cupboard and set it on the bedside table. Putting the phone beside it, I crawled into bed.

Roey jumped up by my feet and settled down, happy to take an afternoon nap. But I couldn't sleep. My head ached and the ringing in my ears seemed louder. Surges of cringing panic washed over me. I huddled under the sheets and peered out the window.

Someone was after me. I knew it in an intense, visceral way I couldn't fathom. My body knew it, more than my mind. I was being hunted.

Outside my bedroom window, the well-loved landscape of my home was ominous. I watched sunlight play on the towering buttresses of the blue gum tree and shivered. The hunter would be comfortable in the bush; he might be there now, in a new blind, watching and waiting. He would know I was alone.

I looked at the gun. I looked at the phone. The dog will bark if she hears anything, I reminded myself. I'll dial 911. I'll pick up the gun. If anyone tries to come through that door I will shoot them.

Try to avoid shooting Blue, the calmer side of my mind quipped.

Right.

Where was Blue? I wished, quite desperately, that he were here with me.

Voices. I started and stared, straining to hear, trying to see. I heard them again, distant voices, calling to a dog, perhaps the neighbors, no threat to me.

My heart was pounding again. I took a deep breath, swallowed, and tried to accept the fear. I thought of what Blue had taught me about fear when I first got on Danny.

Look at what is happening now, Gail. You are sitting in bed. The dog is by your feet. Nothing scary is happening right now. It's all about "what if."

Slowly the hours crept by. Eventually, as the daylight waned, I saw Blue's pickup pulling in the driveway. He got out of the cab bearing a cardboard pizza box, just as he'd promised. Freckles jumped out after him and followed at his heels.

I tried to greet the two of them at the door with a show of normalcy, but it was a dismal failure. Blue took one look at me, put the pizza down, and wrapped his arms around me.

"What happened, Gail?"

Taking him by the hand, I led him to the bedroom. Somehow I felt safer there, away from the big windows. Blue reached to turn on the light, but I stopped him.

"What's the matter?" he said again.

"I saw a footprint." Realizing how inadequate it sounded, I tried again. "A man's footprint. In the brush where it shouldn't have been. Someone's watching me."

Blue looked concerned. Holding my hand in his, he said, "Come on, Stormy. What makes you think this footprint was made by someone who's a threat? Surely there are dozens of possible explanations."

I shook my head emphatically and then winced. "No," I said. "I know it. He's stalking me."

Blue regarded me carefully, as if I were a wild animal he was unfamiliar with. "How do you know it?"

I sighed. "I just do. You think I'm being paranoid, don't you. Because of my concussion."

"Not necessarily. Someone once told me that there are three sorts of illogical thinking. Two are useless and the third is helpful. That's why I asked how you knew."

"So what are my three options?"

"Fear-based thinking, wishful thinking, and intuition."

"Oh," I said. "Well, I guarantee you this isn't wishful thinking. I'm no drama queen."

"That I know." Blue squeezed my hand and smiled. "Do you think it's fear-based or intuitive?"

I thought. "I don't know," I said at last. "I was feeling fearful before I saw the track, it's true. But somehow I just know. My body knows."

Blue nodded seriously. "What does it know?"

"Whoever hit me last night is after me," I said flatly.

"Because?"

"Because I saw him."

"Who is it?" Blue said sharply.

"I don't know. I just know that I know, if you see what I mean. I've been thinking about it all afternoon, lying here in bed. I must have seen him, before he hit me. Jeri said I must have seen the candles, and I don't remember that, either. I must have seen him, too."

"The arsonist?"

"It has to be. Who else would have hit me? I think he ran off because Jeri was pulling in the driveway with all her lights and sirens. Otherwise I'd probably be dead." I shivered.

Blue put his arm around my shoulders and held me close.

"He's after me," I said again. "And I just can't remember. It's all a blank. I've tried and tried. And I still can't."

"I know," Blue said soothingly. "Concussions can be like that."

"It's happened to me before. Once when I was in a car wreck, once when I got bucked off a horse. Both times I couldn't remember anything that happened in the last few minutes before I got knocked out."

"It's pretty common."

"But this time it's important. I've got to remember. I've got to."

"You can't force it, Stormy. It'll come when it's ready, or not at all."

As I opened my mouth to speak, the phone rang. I picked up the receiver.

"Hello."

"It's Jeri Ward. Guess what?"

"What?"

"Those two guys you told me to check on. Hans Schmidt and John Romero? Well I did. You're not going to believe it."

"Try me."

"They both have records."

"Of what?"

I could hear the smile in Jeri's voice. "Arson."

TWENTY-THREE

Shit. Both of them. I don't believe it." I was shocked.

"Well, you must have suspected something," Jeri said. "You told me to run their records."

"I heard about Hans' animal rights past," I said. "But John Romero. I had no idea."

"It's true. Hans Schmidt was indicted as part of a group that burned down a barn and a lab at a research facility. John Romero's story is a little more complicated."

"So what is it?"

"He was a juvenile," Jeri said, "and the records are supposed to be sealed, but in a case like this, where there's a real need to know, I was able to pull a few strings. So this isn't common knowledge."

"All right."

"John Romero was known to have set two wildfires as a teenager. The story's a strange one. It seems his mother had three children, all boys, by three different men. She was never married and she had no steady source of income; apparently she raised these three kids more or less on the street."

"She was homeless?"

"That's right."

"Around here?"

"No. In Southern California. Anyway, our boy John was the oldest son and at a certain point in his teens, he was apparently more or less running wild. Literally. He stole food for his mother and brothers, and from what I understand, he also hunted for it."

"Hunted?"

"That's right. He snared rabbits and quail; he even shot deer with a bow and arrow."

"In Southern California?"

"In the hills," Jeri said. "He claims the fires he started were accidents. They were campfires that got out of hand. He says he was cooking food for his family."

"Wow."

"Yeah. The arresting officers didn't entirely buy this explanation, but they couldn't disprove it. And he was a juvenile. And, obviously, in a tough spot. His probation officer helped him to make a new start, and as we know, he went on to college and vet school, and he's been clean ever since. So the records were sealed."

"Geez." I was thinking of John Romero's dark, sulky glare, and my shrink's words about men and their mothers. "What was his mother like?" I asked Jeri.

"A total loser. Arrested numerous times for prostitution, drug use, and vagrancy."

"I'm amazed she could hang onto the kids."

"She didn't, in the end. The younger two were put in foster homes, eventually."

"Poor kids," I said. Inwardly I was adding two plus two and coming up with big, flashing danger signs. Bad mother, arson record, obvious hostility to women, my God. And a hunter.

"Got to go," Jeri said. "Just thought I'd check in. How are you?"

"Not so good. My ears ring, my head hurts, and I'm dizzy." I thought about telling Jeri about the footprint and my fear, but rejected the idea. If Blue had a hard time believing me, Jeri would think I was crazy for sure.

I hung up the phone after Jeri promised to stay in touch, and recounted what I'd learned to Blue.

"Do you think John Romero hit you?" he asked.

I closed my eyes. My head spun; in the whirling darkness I

tried to find a face. I thought of John Romero. There was nothing. Not the faintest vestige of an image. Nothing.

I thought of Hans. Still nothing. But my mind kept circling back to John. John and his hostility.

"What are you seeing?" Blue asked.

"Nothing. I try, and I have the sense there's something there, but no image will come. I just keep thinking about John."

"Anything special about him?"

"No. But there's something. Something I'm forgetting. Damn. This is so frustrating."

"Come on," Blue said. "Don't get stuck. Maybe a little food will jog your memory." Taking my hand, he pulled me gently to my feet. "Let's go eat pizza."

I held back. "Blue, I don't exactly know how to put this, but I'm scared to go out in the other room and turn on the light. Anyone who's outside can see in so clearly."

Blue gave me a long, steady look. "Stormy, I'm here with you. Anyone who wants to get to you will have to kill me first. And I'm not that easy to kill."

"A bullet would do it," I retorted.

"Sure," Blue said easily. Glancing at my gun on the bedside table, he grinned. "Then you'll have the advantage."

"It's not funny," I protested.

"I know," he said soothingly. "But do you really want to keep hiding in your room?"

"No," I admitted, "I guess I don't."

"Then, here we go." Pulling me to him, he brushed my hair with his lips, and led me out the bedroom door.

Plied with pizza and kisses, how could I resist? I went with Blue, but the fear remained. I glanced nervously at the dark windows for the rest of the evening, and lying next to Blue in bed, I could feel fear curled in my gut, as surely as Roey was curled by my feet.

Someone was hunting me.

I awoke to fear; Blue's presence couldn't dispel it. All morning long, through coffee, breakfast, and chores, I struggled with my anxiety, which seemed to take the form of endless questions. Who was after me? Why couldn't I remember? What in the hell was I going to do?

As I leaned on the arena fence and watched Blue lope Danny, my one thought was how to avoid being left alone. Danny carried Blue smoothly and obediently; the colt slid to a perfect stop when Blue said whoa. I should have been happy. Instead I stayed obsessed with my own inner turmoil. The constant headache and din in my ears seemed part of this extreme whole-body panic. I jumped as my eye caught a bright red car driving up my driveway.

Clay, I realized a second later. Clay Bishop, driving his red Porsche. My overwhelming anxiety was instantly replaced by a new nervousness. How would Clay and Blue deal with each other?

Blue was just unsaddling Danny and looked a question my way.

"Clay Bishop," I said briefly.

Blue nodded and led Danny off to his pen. Clay parked his car and got out.

"Hi, Gail." Clay's easy smile was smoothly in place. Staring after the departing forms of Blue and Danny, he said, "Your new horse?"

"That's right."

"And your new boyfriend?"

"Yep." What else was there to say? I looked at Clay through the cacophony in my mind, and wondered what he was here for.

As always, Clay seemed to intuit my thought. "I came to see if you needed help." Looking at Blue, he added, "but I guess I'm not needed."

"That's nice of you," I said. "How'd you hear?"

"Your friend Detective Ward was out at the barn yesterday. She told me what happened."

"Was she investigating?" I asked curiously.

"That, and riding her horse. I think she was killing two birds with one stone." Clay smiled. "She rides that little gelding almost every weekend. He sure is a funny-looking horse."

I smiled, too. "ET, the extra-terrestrial. The name sure fits him, doesn't it?"

"Yeah, it does. He's got that long skinny neck and those short legs and he's blind in one eye." Clay shook his head. "But he does seem to be as gentle and sweet as they come. Anyway, Jeri was riding him, and she talked to me and Bart and some of the other boarders. She let me know you had a pretty bad concussion. How are you feeling?"

"Not the greatest. I'm hanging in there. I've got a headache."

"I'm sorry to hear that. What happened?"

"What did Jeri tell you?"

"Just that you'd been hit over the head."

"I seem to have caught the arsonist in the act at Judith Rainier's place," I said.

"Really. Did you see him?"

"If I did, I don't remember."

"Wow. If there's anything I can do, let me know." Clay sent a significant look at Blue, who had put Danny away and was headed back toward us. "Though it looks like you've got it covered."

In another minute the two men were shaking hands. They'd met before, I knew. "You remember each other?" I said lamely.

Mutual nods and polite smiles. Damn, this was awkward.

Blue seemed content to stand quietly by my side, and I hadn't a clue what to say next. Clay took the lead.

"I just stopped by to see how Gail was doing," he said. "Mom and Bart send their regards."

"Thank you," I said.

"Take good care," Clay said, seeming to address the comment to Blue and me equally. "I'll see you later."

Folding his long, slender body back into the red sports car, he gave us a jaunty smile and a wave and departed.

As he disappeared down the drive, Blue said, "Poor guy."

"Why's that?"

"I've got you, and he doesn't." Blue pulled me to him and gave me a long kiss. "Lucky me."

"I don't know that you're so lucky. Playing nursemaid to a grouchy sick person."

"Stormy, any man who gets to sleep with you is lucky." Blue smiled. "Real lucky."

TWENTY-FOUR

Monday morning I went to the clinic. Blue protested, but I was sure. No way was I spending the day at home alone. Work felt infinitely safer. Blue promised to be back home before me, and seemed to understand my need not to be left alone. I was grateful.

In one short weekend I seemed to have metamorphosed from a reasonably independent, confident woman into an extreme stereotype of a clinging vine. Here I was, begging my man not to leave me alone. It wasn't exactly the version of myself I would have chosen to present to Blue Winter.

Amazingly, he seemed to accept me in this role, even respect me, as though my behavior were perfectly natural under the circumstances. I wondered how I had ever managed to get so lucky.

Now I stood before Jim, doing my best to sound competent and coherent. "I've got a concussion, but I can function," I told him. "It's just a headache."

Jim looked dubious. Since I didn't exactly want to go into what would sound like paranoid delusions, I didn't mention my fear of being alone at home. "You work when you have a headache, don't you?" I added.

"Whatever you think, Gail," Jim said at last. "You're the judge."

"I'll be careful." What I didn't say, as I went out the back door, was that I had another reason to be here. John Romero's pickup had just passed the glass office door, en route to the rear parking lot. I wanted to see John.

That is, I wanted to see John in a safe situation, with plenty of other people around. I also wanted to see him in reasonable privacy, so we could talk. The parking lot seemed ideal.

I exited the office just as John got out of his truck. My heart began thumping as I walked toward him. What would I see, when my eyes met his? The face I'd last seen in Judith's barn?

The moment, when it came, was anticlimactic. John stopped, as I stood in his path, and looked at me. I stared back at him. Those dark, sulky eyes were familiar, yes, but there was no particular jolt of emotional resonance. If my mind knew something about his face, it wasn't telling.

"Hi, John," I said.

"Hello." John regarded me curiously. I wondered if my inner din was somehow audible. "How are you feeling?" he asked.

"How did you know?"

"Someone told me."

"Who?"

John gave me an unfriendly look. "Detective Jeri Ward, if you need to know."

"Oh."

"She spent a good part of yesterday picking my brain. I think she thinks I bashed you over the head. And lit a few fires."

"Oh," I said again.

"Is that what you think?"

"Uh," I floundered, startled by his blunt approach.

Once again, I saw a brief flash of some very hot emotion in his eyes. "If you think that, you're wrong. Both of you. I may not like you, boss, but I'd never hit you over the head." John made as if to walk around me.

"What about the fires?" I said.

"What fires?" He threw it over his shoulder.

"The fires you set when you were a kid."

Slowly, very slowly, John turned back to face me. "How do you know about that?"

I flinched. "I swore not to tell anyone. And I haven't. Not Jim. Not anyone."

"What do you know?"

"That you were arrested for arson as a kid."

A long, long moment of silence. "Did they tell you what happened?"

"Not really."

"I never set any fires on purpose," he said. "They were just campfires that got away."

"You were cooking food?"

"That's right. A rabbit I'd snared."

"For dinner?"

John met my eyes. "Yeah. For dinner."

Once again, we stared at each other in silence.

"Your mother—" I began.

"You keep your mouth off my mother, boss. I mean it. I won't put up with it. She did what she could and I do not have to hear shit from you."

"I didn't mean—"

"Shut up." Anger blazed up, full force. He shoved his face in front of mine. "She's my mother, damn you."

My eyes were riveted to his scorching-hot eyes; my ears roared, my head spun. Enough rage here to light a hundred barns on fire. In another second it was gone; the dark eyes were as quiet and surly as ever. John looked abashed and stepped back.

"I'm sorry," he said roughly. "It's not something I can talk about."

"I understand." My heart was drumming as if I'd run a marathon. "I'm sorry, too."

This time, when he turned to go, I let him.

Whew. My head was throbbing. I put a hand against the wall to steady myself. My God.

After a minute had passed and my breath came more quietly, I followed John into the clinic.

Nancy met me at the door. "Ellen Weaver has a severely lame horse and she wants you to come right away. She says he had a nail in his foot yesterday and she pulled it out, but today he's worse than ever."

"All right. Tell her I'll be right there."

Ellen Weaver was my only client who boarded her horse out at Quail Run Ranch. Since the place was run by Hans Schmidt's daughter, Jeanie, most of the boarders, with plenty of encouragement from the proprietor went with Hans for their vet work.

Quail Run Ranch, when I arrived, looked even more depressing than usual. In theory, running a large herd of horses out on several hundred acres ought to have been a pretty sight. In practice, however, it was anything but.

Everything out at Quail Run looked neglected. What was left of an old barn was falling down and no longer in use; the barbed wire fences sagged and swayed and were virtually flat on the ground in places. Precious little grass was left to cover the dusty pasture, and what there was of it was brown and dry. I couldn't see the big horse herd anywhere, which wasn't surprising, as the ranch covered a small range of rolling hills, but the gelding who was waiting for me with his owner looked as sad as the place.

I'd been Drummer and Ellen Weaver's vet for almost seven years now, which was perhaps the explanation for her loyalty to me in the face of Jeanie Schmidt's opposition. Jeanie herself was waiting with Ellen, I was less than pleased to see.

The two women stood side by side, the horse on a lead line between them. Jeanie Schmidt was about my own age, Ellen Weaver some ten years older. Both women looked remarkably alike, rounded and soft, with short, neat, blondish gray hair and a little too much makeup. Though both were involved with horses, neither was in any sense an experienced horsewoman.

I got out of my truck slowly, trying to compose myself over the din in my ears and the perpetual headache, which painkillers seemed to dim but couldn't relieve.

"Hi, Ellen," I said. "Hi, Jeanie."

The women greeted me, warmly on Ellen's part and coolly on Jeanie's, but I barely noticed. I was staring at Drummer.

A Quarter Horse–type gelding of about 15.3 hands, Drummer was a bright bay with four high white socks and a blaze; he reminded me a little of my horse, Gunner, though Drummer lacked the blue eye. He had the same bright, inquisitive expression though, and the same playful attitude, a manner that had caused my old boyfriend, Lonny Peterson, to nickname Gunner "Clown."

That is, Drummer had once appeared to me in this way. Now he was thin as a rail, every rib showing, his coat rough, and his eye dull. He was standing on three legs and pointing the toe of his right front foot, which was obviously too painful to bear any weight. He looked terrible.

Neither his owner nor Jeanie seemed aware of this. Ellen chatted to me in a friendly fashion and Jeanie made desultory comments, and both of them appeared oblivious to Drummer's state.

My examination revealed a deep puncture wound in the horse's right front sole, and Ellen told me she'd used a pair of pliers to remove a very large rusty nail from that foot the day before. It had been driven in at least two inches, she said.

I explained to her that such a puncture wound could be really serious, took the horse's temperature and confirmed he was running a fever of 103 degrees, took X rays that showed no structural damage, blocked the foot so that the horse felt no pain, and used my hoof knife to dig out at the wound so it could drain. Then I wrapped the foot with bandaging materials, gave the horse IV antibiotics and painkillers, informed Ellen she'd need to soak the injured hoof in hot water and Epsom salts at least once a day and rewrap it, and that Drummer would need antibiotics in both his breakfast and his dinner for at least ten days. After that I handed her the bill.

Ellen Weaver stared at me in disbelief. "How am I going to do all that? I don't have time. And he's just turned out here in this pasture. How can I catch him, or give him the antibiotics?"

Jeanie looked over Ellen's shoulder at the bill and sniffed. Ostensibly to Ellen, but quite audibly, she whispered, "My father would have charged you half of that. And you really don't need to do all that. It's overkill. Nature will heal this horse."

I saw red. Literally, for a second. I closed my eyes and through the constant roar in my head I seemed to see flashes of red light. Enough was enough.

"Ellen, haven't I been your vet for seven years?" I demanded.

"Yes." Ellen looked startled.

"Have you found me trustworthy."

"Well, yes."

"Then listen to me here, because I'm going to give you a piece of truth. I don't care if you want to use Hans Schmidt as your vet. It doesn't bother me at all. I don't even really care if you renege on your bill. But I do care what you do to this horse."

I put a hand on Drummer's shoulder. "This is a nice horse and I've known him a long time. He's been good to you. When you bought him you were a beginner and he never gave you any trouble. He pretty much taught you to ride. There are a lot of horses who wouldn't have taken care of you like that. In my view, you owe this guy one.

"Now look at him, really look at him. He looks terrible."

I ran my hand over the gelding's rib cage. "You shouldn't be able to see his ribs like this. And look at his hair coat. I don't know who convinced you to turn him out here, or what Jeanie and her dad have been saying about Nature's ways, but this horse is not getting enough to eat. He needs hay twice a day, and maybe a little grain, at this point.

"And trust me on this one. Your horse does need the regime I just described to you if you want him to recover and be sound. A horse who gets injured like this in the wild will often die of it. *That's* Nature's way. If you can't get him doctored here, then move him to a stable where you can keep him in a pen for a while. Take care of him. Feed him, for God's sake."

I took a deep breath. Both the women were staring at me with big eyes, as if I'd suddenly turned into a raging lunatic. Maybe I had. I knew, I really knew, that launching off into an angry tirade was not the way to convince a client to treat a horse properly. I simply hadn't been able to help myself.

After a moment I dropped my eyes from the two shocked

faces. "I'm sorry," I said. "He *does* need the treatment. I guess I'll be going."

As I turned away, I could hear Jeanie's sibilant whisper. "Call my dad. I'm sure he'll help. He's really wonderful."

I got in my truck with angry tears filling my eyes. I hadn't done that poor horse a bit of good, I was sure of it. I'd only alienated Ellen Weaver, a longtime client. Just how stupid could I be? Perhaps this concussion really was affecting my judgment. Staring unseeingly through the windshield as I drove, I imagined that Ellen was even now calling Hans Schmidt to come out and have a look at her horse.

I let my mind dwell on Hans awhile. Hans with his flashy looks, fit body, constant rhetoric. Rhetoric that had, in the past, apparently led to action. Could Hans be the arsonist? Was Hans stalking me?

Nothing came to my mind. No image, no intuition. Only a memory. Hans himself had told me that he trained by running the deer paths through these hills. And he lived only a few miles away from me. It would have been a simple thing for Hans Schmidt to have made his way through the brush to my place. And, for that matter, to have left Judith's barn in the dark, on foot.

Hans was more than athletic enough and very familiar with the trails. But then, I reminded myself, John Romero had once hunted animals for food. I wondered where John lived.

After a minute, I called the office. Nancy had set me up with two more calls. A horse in Watsonville who had been intermittently lame for a week and a recheck on Angie Madison's mare, Sugar.

"Where does John live?" I asked her.

"In Harkins Valley somewhere," she said, sounding surprised. "I can look the address up for you, if you want."

"That's okay," I said hastily.

I hung up the phone with the feeling of having forgotten something important looming large in my mind. What, I asked myself, what? But no answer presented itself. Just that sense that there was something, something there.

I diagnosed the horse with the intermittent lameness as having a small stone trapped between the shoe and the hoof. When this was confirmed by the simple expedient of pulling the shoe, I got a large smile and a clap on the back from the owner, a hearty-seeming man in his sixties.

"I thank you, Doc. I thought it would be something bad like navicular, for sure."

I smiled back, pleased to be the bearer of good news rather than bad for once. Fifteen minutes later, I was pulling into the Bishop Ranch driveway, looking for Angie.

Automatically it seemed, my eyes went to Clay's house. His pickup was gone; the little sports car sat neatly covered in the driveway. Clay was most likely off at work. The big dually pickup Bart drove seemed to be absent also.

There was a blue truck with a matching horse trailer hitched to it sitting in the dirt parking lot, however, and after a minute Angie Madison emerged from a nearby shed row, leading Sugar. She tied the mare to the blue trailer as if she belonged there and motioned me in that direction.

Even from a distance I could see that Angie was mad as hell. Her dark, springy curls seemed to wave wildly in all directions as she moved with short, sharp, jerky strides. Everything about her was choppy. Sugar shied violently as Angie passed by, even though the woman seemed to have done nothing overt to startle the horse.

I walked in the direction of the blue truck and crossed my fingers. Something had pissed Angie off, and I sure as hell hoped it wasn't me. I was not in the mood for being bawled out.

For once I seemed to be in the clear. Angie spoke to me in perfectly civil tones, despite the displeasure written all over her face. She wanted to start training Sugar again, she said. She just wanted to be sure the mare's lungs were clear.

I listened carefully and verified that all seemed well. "Are you going somewhere?" I asked, gesturing at the truck and trailer.

"Just home."

"Oh."

And then, in a rush, as if she couldn't help herself, Angie added, "And away from that asshole, Bart."

"Oh," I said again. It was a well-known fact that Bart's romantic attachments tended to be short and to end badly. Usually his current girlfriend would take offense at some too-obvious flirtation and that would be that.

"Are you and Bart calling it quits, then?"

"I am," Angie snapped. And then, with a mollifying smile, "How about you? Are you still dating Clay?"

"Uh, no."

"Oh. Well for my money, he's the nice brother."

"What happened with you and Bart?" I asked curiously.

"Nothing really. I just got tired of him thinking his shit doesn't stink." Angie sniffed. "Like he was doing me a favor to go out with me. Believe me, I can find another one."

I believed her. "I'm sorry," I said awkwardly. "Must be a hassle, finding a new place for your horse."

"It's no big deal," Angie said crisply. "I live just down the road, right next to Christy George. I can keep Sugar at home. I only brought her here because it was convenient to use the arena to train her."

And to see Bart, I added to myself.

"Thanks, Gail," Angie added.

"Start her out slow, all right?"

"I will. She's too good a mare for me to take a chance."

And Angie loaded Sugar in the trailer and was gone.

I followed her out, staring at Clay's little house as I went. I still couldn't fathom Clay Bishop and what appeared to be his mysterious devotion to me. The nice brother, Angie had said. Something about it was bothersome.

And then my cell phone rang. "Gail, we've got a bad emergency, up in Scotts Valley. A broken leg. Jim and John are both tied up."

"I'll be right there." Immediately I forgot about anything but horses. Horses and their slender, fragile, all too easily damaged legs, which seemed much too insubstantial for such large creatures. Once again I took a deep breath and prayed. "Let this not be too bad. Let me be able to help this horse. Please."

TWENTY-FIVE

Friday morning I awoke at dawn to the crack of a rifle. Heart pounding, I lay next to Blue's quietly sleeping form and trembled. That was a shot. My mind repeated it obsessively, over and over. That was close.

The noise came again, hard and sharp. I jumped out of bed. I knew, even as I moved across the room that the rifle and whoever held it were not on my ridge. My mind had assimilated the sound and found it familiar—just poachers, a mile or so away, perhaps hunting the very buck I had seen last weekend.

The fact that hunting was illegal in these parts did not prevent a few folks from pursuing it, and I often heard rifle shots early in the morning this time of year. I leaned on my window and noticed with surprise that the sky outside was cloudy.

It had been clear and warm for so long that any deviation seemed unheard of. Blue had told me last night that a front was coming in, but I'd rebutted by reminding him of all the other potential fronts that had never materialized.

"This one's for real," he'd said. "It's a cold front. They're predicting thunder and lightning, maybe hail, the whole works."

"I'll believe it when I see it," I told him.

Well, the sky was certainly heavy and gray. I stood in my bare feet and looked out the window while my heart slowed down. I took note that the buzz in my ears, though faint, was still apparent, and that I ached right behind my temples. My symptoms were diminishing, but they were still there.

When I felt calm again, I looked over my shoulder at the bed and Blue. He lay on his back, still asleep, breathing quietly. Quite suddenly, he appeared to me as heroic, noble, a Greek statue of a man. I stared at the way his wavy hair sprang back from his high brow, his straight nose, the strong, square, cleft chin.

Equally suddenly, I was consumed by the urge to touch him. Padding softly to the bedside, I knelt on the floor and pressed my lips to his chest. Breathing in, I trailed my mouth through the fine red-gold hair that covered his skin. I kissed the hollow between his collarbones; I nibbled gently at his shoulder.

Blue opened his eyes. "Hmmm," he said sleepily, and stretched.

I kissed my way across his belly, pulled the covers down, and moved lower.

"Mmmm," Blue said again. "That feels good."

I didn't reply, being otherwise occupied.

Many long minutes later, Blue cradled me in his arms and kissed my mouth. "You are so sweet, Stormy. Now what about you?"

"I'm not feeling too randy these days," I told him honestly. "Something to do with my head hurting all the time, I guess."

"I can imagine."

"It'll come back."

"I know." Blue squeezed me comfortably. "I'm not worried."

"That's good." Disentangling myself from his arms, I stood up. "Looks like you were right about the rain."

We both stared out the window. The sky seemed to be pressing down against the treetops in that dark way that indicated this particular front meant business.

"We might get a little wet," Blue agreed.

"Well, it's sure time." I pulled on my jeans. "And I've got to hurry. I've got a full day today."

An hour later, chores done, I drove out my front gate, sipping coffee from an insulated cup. The boughs of the Monterey pine that arched overhead moved and tossed in the rising wind. Storm coming up.

My mind tossed right along with the branches. Though I felt momentary peace in Blue's company, overriding anxiety crept in as soon as I was alone. The perennial sense that I knew something I needed to remember tormented me. But I could bring up nothing from the depths of my psyche.

Work was my only consolation, work and its constant busyness. While I was occupied with horses I forgot my fear; I even forgot my headache. Being occupied was my respite.

To keep the ever-present tension at bay, I reviewed my scheduled calls as I drove. A mysterious lump on a useful rope horse, a soundness exam on a prospective jumper, a culture on a mare who had absorbed her foal.

And of course, there would be emergencies. There almost always were. And there would be John.

At the thought of John Romero, my heart started to accelerate. This was my constant reaction to the man, to his physical presence or his image in my mind. A rush of adrenaline.

Not for the first time, I pondered what this meant. Was John my assailant? One thing I knew; John was avoiding me with an adroitness that verged on amazing. Considering that we worked in the same office, I barely saw him.

Today looked like no exception. John's truck was in the parking lot when I got to the clinic, and one of the vet trucks was already gone. Nancy confirmed what I suspected. Just like the last few mornings, John had come in early and left on his calls before I arrived.

I was discussing my own calls with Nancy when the phone rang. In another minute, Kelly, the youngest receptionist, ran toward me.

"Gail. There's a bad wreck on Highway One. Up near Davenport. Horses on the road, some are dead. People, too. You've got to go now."

Kelly was too upset to be very coherent, but I got the picture. "I'm on my way."

I drove as fast as the law allowed, headed north of Santa Cruz, on Highway 1. My own fears forgotten, I prayed my usual prayer. Please let this not be too bad. Protect these horses and people from suffering.

I was never sure exactly whom I was praying to. I only knew that the words came—a plea to that which is, a longing for compassion.

Well before I reached the scene of the wreck, I both heard and saw it. Sirens wailed, traffic stopped, up ahead lights flashed red, blue, and yellow. After an indecisive moment, I pulled my truck onto the shoulder and made my way forward. In another minute, I reached a police car.

"I'm a vet," I said. "They called me."

He waved me through.

For a second I had a hard time sorting out the disaster. Cars scattered here and there, twisted and smashed, interspersed with flashing emergency vehicles and uniformed cops, firefighters, and paramedics. Then my eyes caught the sorrel bulk of a horse in the roadway.

The carcass of a horse, my mind corrected. The body lay flat on its side, unnaturally still. And then I saw the other horse.

He was on the shoulder, another sorrel, lying on his belly, with his head up. At a glance, he looked undamaged, but I knew immediately that something was wrong. If he were all right, the horse would be on his feet. It goes against a horse's every instinct to be down in a scene of danger.

A little knot of people stood by the horse. I made my way over. "I'm a vet," I said. "Dr. McCarthy."

"Right," a very young-looking Highway Patrolman answered. "We think this horse was hurt in the crash. He won't get up."

"Is the owner here?"

"We're not sure who the owner is. No one seems to know. These neighbors say they don't recognize the horses. They don't know where they came from. They were loose on the highway apparently."

I looked from face to face. Two older men, three women, several young men. No one said anything. The twisted cars on the road, surrounded by emergency personnel, told their own story. Big-time lawsuits. If one of the people gathered here owned these horses, he or she was keeping quiet. Horses loose on a public roadway made the owner liable.

"Right," I said. "Let's have a look at him."

The sorrel horse lay there quietly, but his gums were pale and there was sweat on his neck. His pulse and respiration were very elevated. Not good.

"Let's get him up," I said.

"He doesn't want to," the young cop replied.

"We'll lift him." I got a halter from my truck and put it on the horse's head.

Several more cops came forward. I pulled on the lead rope and clucked to the horse; the young men set their shoulders against him and pushed. In another minute he was standing.

His right hind leg dangled, swinging freely. I palpitated it gently, though I knew what the outcome would be.

"It's broken up high," I said. "I'm afraid he needs to be euthanized." I stroked the horse's neck.

The young cop who had spoken to me first stepped forward and took hold of the lead rope. "Go ahead and do it."

"All right."

I went to my truck, got the syringe, and filled it. Strange, disjointed thoughts floated through my mind. I seemed to be doing this so much lately. Was this all my life was about, killing horses?

Come on, I chided. Relieving this horse's suffering is a good thing to do. You didn't cause his injury.

But I still felt responsible somehow as I carried the kill shot toward the animal. Along with the rest of humanity, I had created this world of hurtling steel, so alien to horses.

Even as I injected the shot and felt the horse slowly settle, I longed to undo the damage, unmake the world, create a space of peace and harmony where a horse would not come to such an end. As I stood blinking back tears, I saw the stretcher with an ominously covered figure being loaded into the ambulance.

Or a person, I thought. Why must so much suffering be?

For a second the young cop met my eyes and I knew we were reading each other's minds. "It's too bad," he said.

I felt a cold wind riffle through the gray clouds above us. "Yeah," I said. I didn't have any words to offer him.

"Thanks," he added.

"No problem."

I walked to my truck and got in, shut the door, started the engine, and drove away, all without a clue as to how I was doing it. I could feel my head throb; I could hear my ears making a tinny whine.

"I am so tired," I said out loud.

Tired or not, more calls waited for me. The horse with the lump turned out to have pigeon fever. I had to flunk the prospective jumper. Though sound, his X rays showed incipient ringbone. Neither the buyer nor the seller was happy with me.

By the end of the day, I was more tired than ever. At six-thirty, as I was headed home, my cell phone rang. The voice of the answering service operator was brisk.

"A Jeri Ward says ET is colicked."

"Damn. I'll be right there."

"He's at the upper barn, the client says."

"Right."

Shit. I'd forgotten I was on call this evening. I peered through my window at the darkening sky. Great gusts of wind swept across the landscape, bending the trees and beating the thin brown grass flat. It looked as if it were about to start pouring any minute.

Poor Jeri. ET was her first horse, and she was very fond of him, I knew. I stepped on the gas. It would take me at least twenty minutes to reach the Bishop Ranch.

The sky grew colder, grayer, and darker as I drove; the wind rattled against the truck. Occasional drops hit my windshield, but it wasn't really raining yet. Soon, though.

I hoped ET's colic wasn't too bad. I hoped I would get a chance to talk to Jeri about the arson investigation. It had been awhile since we spoke.

More rain splattered against the windshield as I pulled into the Bishop Ranch. Dusk was verging on dark. I could see no one around. Rolling the window down, I shivered as a blast of chilly rain whipped against my face. Simultaneously, a clap of thunder sounded in the distance.

I peered out my window at the empty barnyard. The upper barn, the operator had said. I remembered the place. Above the ranch house.

My headlights cut a path through the gathering rain. Their beams showed me the ranch house, and then farther on, the narrow road that led past the pasture and the upper barn. I reached the driveway, pulled in, parked my truck, and got out. Lights were on in the barn; I walked forward through a tunnel of arching branches that whipped and tossed in the cold wind.

Peering through the darkness, I looked for the forms of Jeri and ET. Next to me a twig snapped. I turned sharply and my head exploded.

TWENTY-SIX

I came to in darkness. Blinking my eyes, I was aware of myself as a presence, nothing more. My head hurt. Slowly pain in blackness evolved into dawning consciousness.

I remembered myself. I knew who I was; I knew what had happened. And I knew, beyond a shadow of a doubt, who had hit me.

Not that I had seen him. Not this time. But something had jolted free in my brain, and I remembered his face, arm raised to strike, in Judith's barn.

I turned my head. I was lying flat on my back with my hands together on my belly. I tried to separate my wrists and couldn't do it. Eventually I realized they were tied together. As were my feet. I turned my face from side to side. The prickly feel and sweet green smell of alfalfa were unmistakable. I was lying on hay.

The darkness, which had initially seemed absolute, was lighter when I turned my face to the right. After a minute, I made out the shape of an open doorway, with a disturbed milky light filtering through it. Moonlight.

There was noise, too. A steady drumming sound. Rain. Rain

on the roof. And loud squeaks and creaks. Something rattled overhead.

I was in a barn, I thought. It was storming outside. As if in confirmation, I caught a greenish flash of lightning in the corner of my eye. A few seconds later, thunder boomed out.

I was pretty sure what barn I was in. But I wondered why I was alive. My assailant meant to kill me; I was sure of it. Why had I been left here?

At the thought, the hairs on the back of my neck lifted in primitive dread. Time to do something.

Slowly and carefully, I explored the material that tied my wrists together. Baling twine, it felt like. Not terribly tight, either. As if my hands had been hastily bound.

Why, I wondered again.

But even as my mind indulged itself in speculation, my hands fumbled restlessly, intuitively. I touched the edge of my right-hand jeans pocket with one finger. There was a knife in that pocket.

Could I do it? I moved my bound arms to the right, shifted and twisted my wrists to put as much slack as possible into the twine. The fingers of my right hand burrowed into the pocket. I could feel the smooth metal surface of the knife. Delicately, gently, I curled my index and middle fingers around it and worked it up. No room for error, here.

I tried not to think about it, tried not to imagine what a fumble would cost me. Letting my fingers move, I kept my mind away from the what-ifs.

The knife was out of the pocket and in my right hand. I thanked God from the bottom of my heart that I had thought to buy a one-handed knife.

The motion was as familiar as breathing; I used the knife every time I had to cut the twine on a bale of hay. Sweetly, easily, the blade folded out. Gingerly I maneuvered it until the sharp edge was against the twine that encircled my wrists. Taking as firm a grip on the handle as I could manage with the fingers of my right hand, I moved my left wrist to saw the twine against the blade.

The knife was sharp. In less than a minute I could feel the twine begin to give. In another second it snapped; I pulled my hands apart. Instantly I sat up.

For a second my head spun, but I blinked and things seemed to settle. I bent forward and cut the twine that bound my feet.

Time to go. I could hear rain battering the walls of the barn; great gusts of wind made the boards creak. A clap of thunder boomed in the distance.

I got to my feet. My head spun again and I swayed. Putting a hand out to steady myself, I touched the rough wood of the wall, then made my way toward the doorway.

As I neared it, I could feel the wind blowing in, spattering my face with raindrops. I shivered. My shirt was damp. No time for that now. I peered out. Despite the rain and clouds, moonlight illuminated the scene with a faint glow. A full moon, I remembered, though I couldn't see it.

I stared at the blowing rain in front of me. Tree branches tossed and flung themselves above a dirt road. I blinked. So where was my truck?

I'd parked it right there. I stared. There was nothing. Just the dark road, the rain, the blowing, black trees. The truck was white; I should see it.

It was gone. He'd moved it, I realized. Moved the so-incriminating evidence of my presence. That was why I'd been left in the barn, to be dealt with later. He needed to move the truck.

Once again, fear rose up. He'd be back. He'd be back to kill me.

I took a deep breath. Putting my head down, I ducked out into the rain and started running down the hill. I'd go to the boarding stable, find someone, find help. Rain blew into me, soaking through my shirt, through my hair. I raised my head, trying to see, and came to a dead stop.

A figure was coming up the road toward me. Completely clad in a slicker and rain hat, his features were invisible in the pouring rain and darkness. But I knew who he was. In every atom of my body I recognized my enemy.

I turned and ran back the way I had come. As I neared the barn, I saw what I hadn't seen from inside the doorway. Two horses were tied under a lean-to roof on one side. A saddled horse and one with a pack rig. Freddy and Blackjack.

I didn't think, just went with my first instincts. Slowing to a walk, I stepped toward Freddy. His eyes were big, but he held his ground. Untying him, I pulled the reins over his head with one hand and swung up.

In another second I whirled the horse to face my assailant. Through a haze of rain, I could see the slicker-clad figure lift his arm in the classic pose of a man sighting along the barrel of a pistol. Moonlight gleamed on metal. In the split second it took me to assimilate this, I dug my heels into Freddy's ribs; the horse leaped forward just as the shot cracked out.

I kicked the horse again as he bounded; startled by the noise, he needed little encouragement to run. Grabbing the saddle horn and a handful of mane, I clung on as he lunged up the hill.

Downhill was the direction of people and help, but that slicker-clad figure stood between me and safety. I ducked low over Freddy's neck as another shot rang out. Almost instantly it was swallowed up in a clap of thunder.

Freddy was bolting in earnest now. I twined my fingers in his mane; my feet fumbled for the stirrups. Rain lashed my face, ran down my cheeks, dripped off my hair. Blinded and gasping, I could barely stay with the stampeding animal. But the alternative was a good deal worse.

On we went. Upward, ever upward. Uphill, as far as I remembered, was only empty woods. Wind whipped my ears and roared in the trees around me. I tried a tentative pull on the reins and felt Freddy respond. My feet found the stirrups; thanking God they were roughly the right length, I sat up a little straighter and took a good hold of the reins. Freddy slowed. I pulled again and he came down to a trot.

Even as I checked him to a halt, a great gust of wind and rain broadsided us like an openhanded slap. Freddy flung his head and switched his tail; I tried to shake my wet bangs out of my eyes. Turning the horse around, I looked back down the hill.

Between the darkness and the storm, I could see little, only dark trees in a noisy, blowing tangle. I stared. Freddy's ears came up and he stared, too.

Then, simultaneously, lightning flashed and the horse neighed. In the brief eerie light, I saw what Freddy's more accurate senses had already registered—a horse, galloping up the hill after us.

A horse and rider, I realized. Even as thunder clapped out, I spun Freddy and kicked him back into a gallop. I recognized the pursuing horse's blaze face. Blackjack. The slicker-clad horseman was clinging to the pack rig, desperate to catch us. I already knew he carried a gun.

Freddy drove forward, propelled by his own adrenaline as much as my cue. I leaned forward over his neck, thanked God he was surefooted and bold. Despite the wild storm buffeting us up the steep hill, the horse charged as if in the front line of a battle.

I rode. Now we were in the eucalyptus grove, the tall trees groaning and creaking as they swayed over us. Lightning flashed on the ridge, showing me the forest of pale trunks and branches, writhing and twisting. I gripped the saddle horn in one hand and the reins in the other and thumped my heels into Freddy's sides.

Rain blew in my face; wind dinned in my ears. The whole world was a dark, noisy kaleidoscope. Desperately, I tried to think. What to do? As far as I knew, this dirt road led only to the clearing on top of the ridge. And if I reached it—what then? Go back, of course. By the trail. Back to civilization, to help and safety.

Swiping the water out of my eyes with one hand, I gasped as the horse stumbled. Automatically I grabbed at the horn; Freddy recovered himself in one stride and galloped on. I didn't dare risk a look back. I kept my attention forward; I rode for all I was worth. I knew he was back there, but I knew also that I could go faster than he could. Riding on a pack rig would be difficult at the best of times and an all-out gallop in a rainstorm was hardly the best of times.

It seemed to take forever. I twined my fingers in the wet, dark strands of Freddy's mane, tried to stay balanced and forward over the horse's shoulders, where he could most easily carry me. Clucking to him rhythmically, I tried to encourage him in this strange pandemonium we'd both been thrown into. Once again I thanked God he was tough.

Soon, I thought, soon we'd be there. Lightning crackled on the ridge again; I could see we were nearing the top. In another minute we crested the hill; the clearing opened up around me. In the corner of one eye, I saw the dark bulk of the huge blue gum tree. I pulled Freddy to a jerky, prancing stop.

Back, I thought, go back. But which way? Down the trail? I didn't know which route the killer had taken. I had spotted him before the trail branched off. Or at least I thought so.

If I went the wrong way, I'd meet him point blank. And he was carrying a gun.

Freddy threw his head and danced impatiently as I dithered. Eucalyptus trees moaned and squealed as the storm flung their branches above me. I blinked more water out of my eyes and tried desperately to think.

Which way to go? I stared at the wildly tossing crown of the big blue gum, barely visible in the darkness. Which way to go?

Another crackle of greenish light flashed around me, with a strange sizzling noise. The hair on my arms stood up. Instantaneously thunder boomed, deafening me. Freddy reared.

"That was too close," I gasped.

As if somehow cued, the wind increased its fury and the rain, already icy, began to sting. Hail. My God. I could hear it rattling on the eucalyptus leaves. Freddy jumped forward, tossing his head and fighting the bit. I heard another loud crack.

Not thunder. I looked up and saw him, right where the road opened into the clearing. Blackjack's white blaze gleamed in the faint light, not twenty feet from me. The horseman was shooting from his back.

Freddy plunged toward his stable mate, bulling through the bridle, ignoring my tugs. I saw the slicker-clad form on the horse point the pistol right at me. I closed my eyes.

Please help me, I prayed. And everything exploded in an overwhelming crash.

Was I hit? I was still clinging to a wildly whirling Freddy as a huge thud shook the ground. Shit. For a second I could see nothing but waving leaves and twigs. The big blue gum had dropped a branch right between me and Blackjack.

Had he fired at me again? He had, I thought. But the branch had fallen at the same time. And suddenly I knew what to do.

Wrenching Freddy around by main force, I rode around the branch. There he was. Blocking my path again. I took a deep breath and kicked Freddy right at him.

His hand came up; I prayed. He flung the gun right at my head. I ducked and the gun missed me. I was right, I thought, I was right.

Now we were crashing by him, feet away, Freddy charging forward, headed for home. I both heard and glimpsed Blackjack whirl with us. And then the rider was hurtling through the air toward me, arms outstretched for my shoulders in a flying tackle.

I saw him coming; so did Freddy. Even as I twisted, the horse leaped sideways, away from the attacker. I felt the impact on Freddy's rump, felt hands clutch at me. Freddy humped his back and lashed out with both back feet.

I heard a yell and a sharp, smacking noise and looked back over my shoulder. Blackjack, riderless, was right on our heels, and behind him the slicker-clad figure lay motionless on the ground.

I didn't hesitate. Kicking Freddy one more time, I headed down the hill at a long trot, through the blowing storm. I was going home.

TWENTY-SEVEN

Riding down the hill, thoughts coalesced. I knew damn well where I would go first. As I rode, I became aware of how wet I was, and how cold. Adrenaline ebbed; I shivered. My body ached; my head hurt. My shirt and jeans were soaking. My boots were full of water.

Paradoxically, it filled me with rage. *Damn him to hell* was the only thought in my mind.

I reached the barn where I'd been tied up and rode on. Past the ranch house, down to the big arena. Here I dismounted and led Freddy through the gate. Blackjack followed. I pulled Freddy's bridle off his head and turned him loose.

"Thank you," I said.

Then I let myself out of the arena and shut the gate. I had some business to take care of.

Wind and rain blew into my face as I marched across the drive and up the steps of Clay's little house. I banged on the door and threw it open.

Clay was sitting in front of the TV; his head jerked around, eyes wide, as startled as if the storm itself had blown the door open and swept in. Water dripped off my clothes and hair and onto the carpet as I stepped into the room. Clay's shocked stare followed me in.

"Gail!"

"That's right," I said, as evenly as I could manage. "Surprised to see me?"

Clay said nothing; his mouth dropped half-open. Dispassionately, I noted that he didn't look particularly handsome at the moment. His lack of chin was all too obvious.

Clay seemed to gather himself. "What happened?" he asked.

For a moment our eyes met; Clay dropped his gaze to my soaking clothes. "What happened?" he asked again.

"What happened," I said, "is, your brother Bart tried to kill me."

"What?"

"However, he didn't manage it and he is now lying in the clearing at the top of the ridge. I don't know if he's dead or alive."

"My God, Gail."

"Don't sound so shocked, Clay. It doesn't cut any ice with me. You knew what Bart was up to."

"Gail, I . . ."

And suddenly my control broke. "You bastard!" I screamed. "What did you plan to do, sit here watching TV while he killed me?"

"Gail, I didn't know."

"The hell you didn't. You knew Bart was the arsonist. You knew he hit me over the head at Judith's. You must have known he planned to kill me."

"I didn't, I swear."

"Oh bullshit, Clay. Would you just for one moment drop your Mister Nice Guy pose and have a look at the truth. You suspected Bart from the beginning."

Clay was silent.

"And," I went on, "you knew, if you let yourself think, that Bart would need to kill me after I caught him at Judith's place."

"But you didn't remember. You said so."

"Bart couldn't count on that. And in the end, I did remember. I saw him, right before he hit me."

Clay and I were both quiet.

"How could you?" I could hear my voice rising. "How could you protest all that devotion and stand by while Bart tried to kill me? What kind of thing are you?"

"Dammit, Gail, I didn't know!" Clay was yelling, too; I saw a brief flash of genuine feeling in his eyes.

I didn't care. "What the hell do you mean, you didn't know?" I shouted at him.

"I didn't know what Bart was doing. I might have wondered, but I didn't know."

"That is the most complete bullshit I ever heard. You suspected Bart the whole time. I thought you were upset when the barn here burned just because it was stressful for your family, but it wasn't that, was it? You were upset because you knew Bart did it."

Clay jumped to his feet. "Will you listen? I didn't know. I wondered."

"Clay." I spoke very slowly and clearly, enunciating each word. "You must have had some reasons for your suspicions. What were they?"

"I saw Bart in the hay barn, about an hour before we noticed the fire here," Clay said miserably. "I was sitting on my porch, drinking a beer. There was a full moon."

"I remember."

"I saw someone moving around in the hay shed, which was at this end of the big barn. I stood up, tried to get a better look; I was behind the bushes in front of my porch. He didn't see me."

"Right," I said.

"Eventually I figured out it was Bart. I recognized his way of moving. So I sat back down and finished my beer. Bart didn't usually go in the hay barn at that time, but he did check on the horses before he went to bed. I didn't think anything of it. He never did see me, sitting there on the porch.

"Then we had the fire, and then, when that detective was questioning all of us, Bart said he hadn't gone in the hay barn."

"So you suspected him."

"I wondered. I thought it was possible I was wrong, that I'd seen someone else. After all, it was dark; whoever it was wasn't using a flashlight."

"Did you have any other reasons to wonder about Bart?"

"I knew he needed money. His ex-wife was after him pretty hard for some child support he never paid her during those years when he was a bum. He borrowed some money from me, but I knew it wasn't enough. I think he tried to borrow some from Mom, but she said no."

"So he burned the barn down for the insurance money."

Clay shook his head. "I think it might have been the only way he could think of to pay his debts. Bart doesn't have anything of his own, you know. Even that truck he drives belongs to Mom."

"What made him think Mom would give him the insurance money?"

Clay shrugged. "She's losing her grip on things. She puts up a good show, but she's actually a lot sicker than she looks. Just lately she's left everything, including the accounts, to Bart."

"Right," I said.

"What in the world was I supposed to do?" Clay turned his face away. "Tell that detective I suspected my brother?"

I was silent.

"I was so relieved when Christy's place burned." Clay winced. "That sounds terrible, but I thought it meant I must be wrong, that it wasn't Bart."

"So when did it dawn on you?"

Clay didn't answer.

"I'll tell you when it dawned on me," I went on. "Or when it should have dawned on me. When Angie told me where she lived. Next to Christy's place. I'll bet Bart set that fire and then picked Angie up and off they went. No one saw him, and no one noticed the fire until he and Angie were safely at some restaurant."

"But why would he?" Clay said desperately.

"For that very reason. The fact that he had no apparent reason.

He needed to direct suspicion away from himself. I don't think Bart knew too much about arson. He thought his own barn fire would be put down to a hot bale of hay. It must have come as a terrible shock to him when that fire investigator wasn't fooled, even for a moment. I think Bart reckoned that if there were another, apparently purposeless arson, suspicion would fall on Marty Martin, or someone like him. And it did."

For a long moment Clay stared right at me. "It's what you think, isn't it?" I demanded.

Clay dropped his eyes.

"So why," I went on conversationally, "do you suppose Bart kept starting fires, once the cops were busy investigating other people? It was a big risk."

Clay continued to say nothing. I kept staring at him. I knew why Bart had done it. Or I thought I knew why.

I remembered what my shrink had told me about arsonists; what Walt Harvey had told me about arsonists. I remembered the dinner scene at the Bishop house, and how constantly Doris Bishop had thrown covertly hostile remarks in Bart's direction. At a guess, this had been going on all of Bart's life.

At another guess, I suspected Bart Bishop hated women, despite his constant show of girlfriends. That love-'em-and-leave-'em pattern was in itself a tip-off to a man who couldn't connect to women.

And how would he know how? I could hear my shrink's voice in my head. If the first essential connection to women is between a son and his mother, then Bart Bishop had clearly been left wanting.

And what of Clay? I glanced at him and caught the strangest expression on his face. It came and went almost instantaneously, but I registered it. As his eyes rested on me, he smiled. A tiny, quick, smug smile. Unbelievably, Clay Bishop was gloating.

The next moment his face showed only appropriate concern, but I knew what I had seen. At some level, perhaps beneath his conscious awareness, Clay was rejoicing in my distress.

Of course, I thought. I had hurt this man deeply. I had chosen his rival over him—the ultimate male insult. Somewhere inside, he was very, very angry at me.

But Clay had trained himself not to show anger. In fact, I suspected that Clay had taught himself not to *feel* anger. Perhaps because there was so much anger buried inside of him. After all, Doris Bishop had raised both Bart and Clay. Maybe both men were equally angry at women. Clay had merely chosen a different way of dealing with his rage. He hid from it.

"She named you well," I said finally.

"What?" Clay looked confused at the change of subject.

"Your mother. You've got feet of clay."

"Gail, I—" Clay began.

I cut him off. "I don't want to hear it. I'm done listening to your nice-guy routine. Bart lit those last two fires because he was frustrated and angry inside, particularly at women. It's no accident that the three fires he started to divert suspicion were all horse barns that belonged to single women who are supporting themselves. I think Bart got his jollies both from the violence of the fires and the attack on women. In some way the act fit his inner needs. Once he took it up, he wanted to keep doing it. But you, Clay, you said you loved me."

"I did, Gail. I thought I did."

I met his big, soft, long-lashed eyes with a sort of horror. As ever, Clay appeared so smoothly nice on the surface. It was only now that I understood that this veneer gave no clue as to what was going on underneath.

"So if you thought you loved me, why were you willing to just sit around after you knew Bart had hit me over the head? Tell me that."

Clay met my eyes, mutely miserable. "I didn't know what to do. I didn't want to believe it was happening."

"So you just kept it all to yourself. Like you do everything else. You did nothing, said nothing."

Clay flinched at my words; in that moment I saw clearly that despite his aura of strength and confidence, inside, where it counted, Clay was abjectly weak. In a very real sense, he was afraid to know himself, afraid to face his real feelings. He had spent his life posturing niceness and competence; it was the only version of himself he was comfortable with. When his life took a turn that didn't fit in with being a "nice guy," Clay was lost.

"What was I supposed to do?" he asked me. "Tell you, 'I think my brother might be a murderer'?"

"Yeah," I said, "something like that. We're talking about saving my life here. I think you should have been willing to sacrifice your brother. I think you should have told the truth."

Once again, our eyes connected. I was aware of my hair and clothes, still steadily dripping onto the carpet; I could feel that the warmth of the house had taken some of my chill away. But my heart was cold. In some way I couldn't fathom, Clay's betrayal cut much deeper than Bart's attempt to kill me. I didn't take Bart's attack personally; I recognized it as his attempt to survive. It was Clay's lack of action that hurt.

"In case you're interested," I went on conversationally, "Bart got me out here on a fake emergency. He must have found out I was on call. He told the answering service he was Jeri Ward; after all, that name could be male or female.

"Once I was at the upper barn, with no one around, he bashed me over the head, again, tied me up and left me in the barn. Then he moved my truck. He was all dressed up in a slicker and rain hat, and he's about my height. No one seeing him from a distance could have known it wasn't me. No doubt he was wearing latex gloves, too.

"I bet he called the answering service and sent 'me' on another fake emergency, somewhere nearby in Harkins Valley. That way, when the truck was found there, it would appear that was where I disappeared. Then he walked back, probably along the trails, so no one would see him. Your brother knows every trail in these hills; he's been riding them all his life.

"You know what he planned to do with me?"

Clay shook his head, not meeting my eyes.

"I'll tell you. I've had a little time to work it out, and I can guess. He meant to shoot me in the head in the middle of one of those thunderclaps and pack my body off into the woods and push it into some ravine. That's why he had Freddy saddled and Blackjack there with the pack rig. With winter just coming on, if he'd chosen the right place, nobody would have found my body for a long, long time. It was a good plan."

I stared at Clay, water still running down my face from my hair. "Bart's only problem was he tied me up in too much of a hurry and didn't take the knife out of my pocket. He was in a big rush to move the truck. So I got away. But I didn't get by him. He saw me and started shooting at me. It was your horse that saved me, Clay."

Clay looked up at that.

"That's right, Freddy saved me. He kicked Bart right in the head, I think. And I remembered that Bart only kept four bullets in his pistol. He told me, that night at dinner. Once I realized he'd shot at me four times, I knew the gun was empty."

Clay shook his head, his eyes back on the floor.

"If I ever hear you're not taking perfect care of Freddy," I went on, "I will personally make sure you get accused of being an accessory in my attempted murder. Do you hear me?"

Clay nodded.

"As far as I'm concerned, as of now, all that I just told you never happened. I'm going to tell Jeri Ward that I remember who hit me in Judith's barn. And I do. I'm going to call the cops now," I said.

Clay's gaze stayed steadily on mine, those eyes as limpid as ever. But I saw only blank, opaque shutters; I no longer had any sense that I knew who Clay was. It occurred to me that I never had known him, only deceived myself into thinking I did. I could read Danny's heart and mind better than I could Clay's.

I walked toward the phone, my eyes locked on Clay. Perhaps I should have been afraid, but I wasn't. Clay never moved.

"If I were you," I said, with my hand on the phone, "I'd go see if Bart's alive or dead. And you'll need to put away Freddy and Blackjack; I turned them loose in the arena."

Clay took a step toward the door, then paused.

For another long second we stared at each other. Then I lifted the receiver, and Clay turned and went out into the rain.

EPILOGUE

Bart Bishop survived. He was in a coma for a week, and a wheelchair for a month after that, but he eventually recovered completely and was able to stand trial.

Clay and I haven't spoken since that night.

And Blue Winter moved his trailer out to my place and has been here ever since.

All in all, a happy ending.

Laura Crum lives in Aptos, California, with her husband and son and a large family of animals. *Hayburner* is her seventh Gail McCarthy mystery.

To find out more about her mystery series, or send her an e-mail, go to http://members.cruzio.com/~absnow.